To Mandi, with Love

by

F. Edward Marx

ISBN 0-9755430-0-8

First printing June 2004

Published by F. Edward Marx Literary Services
PO Box 162
Union Lake MI 48387-0162

Printed in the United States by Morris Publishing
3212 East Highway 30
Kearney, NE 68847
1-800-650-7888

To those I have loved and lost:
I will never forget what we once shared.

Love is patient, Love is kind.
It does not envy, it does not boast, it is not proud.
It is not rude, it is not self-seeking,
It is not easily angered, it keeps no record of wrongs.
Love does not delight in evil but rejoices in the truth.
It always protects, always trusts,
Always hopes, always preserves.
I Corinthians 13:4-7 (NIV)

Table of Contents

Dear Mandi,

I lost my heart to you the first time we met. You were eight-years-old, and had just stepped out of the pool. Standing in front of your mother and me, you shivered off the droplets of glistening water, and whispered, "Mom, I'm really having fun, can I stay and swim a little longer?"

Before you turned to race back to play, I couldn't help notice the open hole at the base of your neck. I asked your mother if that was why you whispered.

She nodded yes, explaining about the tracheotomy through which you breathed. She told me of your birth with throat cancer and your desperate fight for life as a baby. Then, when she told me about the chemo, and the one hundred eighty-odd operations that sacrificed your vocal cords, my heart broke. I felt one-half of it gripped in sympathy for what you endured, and the other half soaring at the miracle of your life. I loved you even then.

Now that you are out of my life, a part of me is missing. I can't be there for you, but I can offer some of the lesson that life has taught me—most of which have come through suffering the consequences of my pride, arrogance, and foolishness.

Mandi, let God guide you through this life. The tumultuous storms of existence are incredibly difficult to negotiate, but to be caught in life's storms without love is like a ship without its rudder, floundering at the mercy of the crashing emotional seas. The eventual outcome is a desperate sinking into selfish need until all that is truly important has been lost.

My selfishness ended up hurting all of the people that I loved, especially you. To be responsible for breaking your innocent heart was a burden that was almost more than I could bear.

Will you forgive me?

I've paid such a dear price for my mistakes. They literally cost me everything. I even lost myself, or at least who I thought I was.

But you know what?

I have found that the greatest sacrifices lead to the greatest rewards. I've also learned that the fire of the soul can cleanse not just destroy. For two years, I burned as if I had swallowed a shovel full of hot coals. Melted of my pride and arrogance, I had no choice but to look at myself in a way that goes beyond this fleshly existence. Then, that flame that seared me to my soul began to change. Instead of a raging emotional inferno, it slowly became a torch that lit the path of self-examination. Eventually, I arrived at the destination of self-discovery and the most amazing thing happened. I found God waiting for me there.

The stories that follow are my journey and the lessons I have learned. Some are humorous, some are insightful, and I hope all are entertaining.

Just maybe you will read this one day and think fondly of me.

The List

I conjured up the list some time ago, however, it didn't mature and become a term used on a daily basis until I bought the lake-house. Having spent every last dime on the down payment, I didn't realize how many things were still needed. This resulted in the simple idea that whenever I thought of something that was required I would...put it on the list. Then, when the items above the one just added were purchased or removed, the new entry moved up, eventually becoming the next item in line.

While this seemed like a reasonable approach to household management, I am compelled to caution you from considering the idea of starting your own list. Once you place pen to paper and the ink flows, the list has the potential to become a life-long obsession that will haunt and harangue you, with the only relief attained by acquiring the one item not on the list—a final resting place.

Once I created the list, I had no choice but to watch it grow. Like Dr. Frankenstein, I longed for the days when I at least felt the illusion of control. Unfortunately, both our creations took matters into their own hands, so to speak.

In the beginning, I managed the list by not letting it expand too quickly, carefully adding only necessities like a new stove or a refrigerator. Inevitably, something else would get added, first a new counter for the kitchen. Then, the counter needed stools. I'm not exactly sure when it happened, but things like a deck appeared, then a boat. Shortly after that, I realized I'd lost control.

The list no longer served to plan or manage; it had matured to a position of dominance and self-perpetuation. When I crossed the big-ticket item of the deck off the list, feeling quite satisfied with a job well done, I found it necessary to immediately add new items. I needed to stain the deck, and mount a gas grill. Of course, the deck had to have new lighting. By crossing off one item, ten others needed to be added. All of a sudden, I realized I had created a creature with a logarithmic appetite that would forever try to dominate daily life.

The list also had the power to coerce others into helping it. I thought it was a special day when we crossed the boat off the list. Little did I know that after I built the dock, I needed fifteen life preservers, ski ropes, a $150.00 tube, knee-boards and an oil refinery; with all you guys telling me: now that we have the boat, we need to put not one, but two jet-skis on the list.

There were a few positive aspects to the list. When some busybody came over and suggested that I needed to remodel the bathroom, I'd just look her in the eye, and with all earnestness say, "That's a good idea, I'll put it on the list."

Of course, I didn't mention that I placed it on the part of the list that I plan to get to some time in the middle of the next century.

The list also provided a safe, no-feelings-hurt, answer when your brother decided that he couldn't live without a new $400.00 video game. He seemed to take it pretty well when I said, "I don't have the money right now, but I can put it on the list."

Whether it ever comes off the list, only time will tell.

Once the new addition made it to the top of the list, it became my true nemesis. I feared even thinking about it. I knew the list had conscripted contractors and sub-contractors, who joyfully wanted to create list and sub-list.   I could feel the list adding things like foundations, heating and cooling, plumbing and electrical, and let's not forget, the list for decorating and furnishing the space yet to be created.

The truly frightening aspect was that any one of those sub-lists had the potential of becoming its own independent list.

The list had become so powerful and all consuming that my days began to unfold something like this: your mother would say, "Good Morning, what do you think about this couch in the new catalog?"

Rubbing the sleep out of my eyes, I said, "It's very nice maybe we should put it on the list." Then the phone rang and it's your sister calling from college, pleading, "I really need a new computer."

All I could say was, "Okay, I'll try to move it to the top of the list."

I hadn't even had a cup of coffee yet and the list was already sailing along in full regalia. I looked in the refrigerator to cook a couple of eggs for breakfast, asking, "Where are the eggs?" Only to hear in reply, "We're out of eggs, you better put some on the list."

There is Wisdom in the Pain

A story circulated through the computer industry for several years. For me, this story epitomized the value of wisdom and what can be learned from one's mistakes.

An engineering executive in charge of developing a revolutionary memory device spent over five million dollars on research and development. His team produced a 50-Megabyte hard drive, something that no other company had been able to accomplish.

Excited about introducing their state-of-the-art technology, the company prepared for the biggest trade show of the year. Needless to say, everyone anticipated an overwhelming response and skyrocketing sales.

During the event a competing company introduced a 60 Mega-byte device. Not only did they steal the promotional thunder, but all the sales as well.

After the trade show, the dejected engineering executive went into the CEO's office and handed him his resignation.

The CEO asked, "What's this?"

"It's my resignation," the executive replied. "I've cost this company five-million dollars and we have nothing to show for it."

The CEO, seeing through the eyes of wisdom and compassion at the heartsick man, said, "I just spent five-million dollars on your education. Do you think I am going to let you go, and give some other company the opportunity to hire you? This is a difficult situation, but I'll be damned if I going to let someone else capitalize off this misfortune. You pull it together, Mister. Get yourself back to work, and show me what you've learned."

Mandi, you knew me as a kind, loving, and decent man, and you loved that man. But I was also selfish and arrogant--two characteristics that God loathes. Those things kept me from the

- 6 -

destiny that He planned for my life.   Pride, arrogance, selfishness, greed, lust, hate and anger are all characteristics that keep each of us from an intimate relationship with a loving Father. A Father who cares for us so deeply that words cannot describe.

The consequences of my mistakes hurt the very people that I loved the most, but it also laid open my soul to a psyche-cleansing, spiritual fire.   That flame consumed the selfishness, burned away my pride, and torched my arrogance; then, from those ashes a new man emerged.

Unfortunately, there are some who can't forgive me.   They have thrown me to the curb like so much of yesterday's garbage. The sad part is that they have paid such a dear price for my education, and it is now that I am most worth knowing.

He Made Me Pick His Nose

I never realized how much I'd miss those stimulating conversations that I used to have with you, Bobby, and Jo Jo. Like the time you came running into my room with your brother chasing close behind. Then, before you could register your complaint, he blurted out, "I didn't make her pick my nose!"

Upon my inquiry, Bobby adamantly denied making you do such a thing.

"Oh Huh!" you indignantly replied. "He made me stick my finger half-way up his nose," emphasizing that fact by wiping your finger on my arm.

I thought I solved the dispute when I told Bobby to stay out of your room. The thought that justice had not yet been served never having occurred to me.

Moments later, I heard your brother screaming, "Ooowww, quit biting me."

Apparently that was the proper measured response for the offense of making someone pick someone else's nose, because by the time I left my chair and walked to Bobby's room the two of you were quietly watching TV together.

Shortly after this I heard the front door slam closed and your sister Jo Jo yelling, "Quick, everybody, come here, you have to see what I have. As I started down the stairs where Jo Jo waited excitedly, I got an unmistakable whiff of pig.

Jo Jo said, "Look what I bought with the fifty dollars I made at the fair today." Then she opened a small cardboard carrying case to expose a little pink livewire, also known as a baby pig. Grinning from ear to ear, Jo Jo exclaimed, "Isn't he adorable."

"Jo what are you doing with that?" I asked.

"He's mine, I bought him, isn't he the cutest thing you ever saw."

"Jo, he's a pig, where are you going to keep him?"

"Here!"

"Here? Where here?"

"In the house, the guy I bought him from said that you can train him to go the bathroom on the toilet."

"Oh yeah, well where do you plan on him going to the bathroom until he figures that out. Jo Jo you made a mistake, you can't keep a pig here. You'll have to take him back."

Jo Jo's eyes began to moisten. "I can't, the guy who sold it to me isn't there any more."

What a surprise, I thought. Not to mention that this type of all sales final was the first thing that made any sense so far. "Let me get this straight, you used the fifty dollars you earned today, and bought this pig thinking you would keep it here in the house."

Tears streamed down Jo's cheeks. "Yes."

Feeling sorry for Jo because she had been taken advantage of, not to mention blowing her hard earned fifty dollars, I realized the baby pig was cute. Unfortunately, Jo Jo didn't realize just how fast baby pigs turn into big pigs. Wondering what type of magazines the pig might like to read while exercising his bowels, I felt I had no choice. "Jo Jo, I'm sorry, you made a mistake. You can't keep a pig, end of discussion."

As she called each of her friends looking for a home for her baby, I had to listen to Jo repeating the teary-eyed tale of the adorable baby pig and the mean old stepfather.

To my astonishment she found the pig a home and actually started talking to me again--about a week later.

Now as I sit here, thinking about what I have lost, and how much I miss all of you, I realized, I will never again hear things like: He made me pick his nose.

The Storm

For some the journey through life is a calm series of years in which they pass through the normal trials and tribulations of this earthly experience. Somehow, they manage to live quiet productive lives, blessedly unchallenged. They are the fortunate ones—or are they?

The rest of us experience periods of tremendous anxiety, stress, emotional pain or grief. My internal storm arrived in a tempest of ceaseless thoughts and feelings that could not be controlled or diminished.

Mandi, I expect that someday those winds of internal hysteria will come along and begin to sweep your thoughts and feelings to and fro. The tempest can be so strong that you will feel like a leaf hurtled along by the intensity of your own emotions. Then when you combine that with the engulfing waves of grief that break against the battered timbers of your heart, you'll find your tiny ship of self in jeopardy of overflowing and capsizing. Left alone to battle through the emotional gale, you will struggle to find a psychological port that might shelter you. You'll look for anything that will block the severe forces that rage within as you try to wall off the pain.

Some people turn to alcohol, some to drugs, some to food, others to sex or gambling. Some seek the solace of others, hoping not to face the storm alone. Others lash out in anger and rage as they try to counteract the winds of torment with a destructive force of their own. And still others succumb to the storm, aimlessly drifting along waiting and hoping that the typhoon will end, as they are blown to the brink of their existence. Unfortunately, you cannot hide forever in whatever mind-altering port you took for shelter. Whether you chose drugs, or alcohol abuse, a codependent relationship, or the isolation of hatred and animosity, sooner or later, you must re-emerge to try to find yourself before becoming totally lost in the dark quagmire of the soul.

When my storm came, I knew I had lost my moral compass. Not only was I flooded by waves of grief and blown by the hurricane of anxiety, but I ended up dashed upon the rocks with the total loss of everything that I valued.

I could find no port from this storm. A river of alcohol did not help. The comfort of others did not console. Anger and animosity only came reflecting back multiplied in its intensity. I was adrift in a sea of pain, and rudderless to steer through the waves of grief. Fearing for my emotional and mental life, I opened the Bible as a last resort. And as no small miracle this story appeared:

And there arose a great storm of wind, and the waves beat into the ship, so it was full.

And He was in the higher part of the ship, asleep on a pillow and they awoke Him and said unto Him. "Master carest thou not that we perish."

And He arose and rebuked the wind and said unto the sea, "Peace be still." And the wind ceased and there was a great calm.

And He said unto them, "Why are ye so fearful? How is it that ye have no faith?"

And the disciples feared exceedingly and said one to another. "What manner of man is this, that even the wind and sea obey Him?"

As I read those words I realized I too was caught in the storm. I opened my heart and cried out. "Help me Lord, carest thou not that I perish."

It was then that the waves of grief ceased and the winds of pain diminished. Then, just like the disciples who were held in fear and awe as to, what manner of man is this? I too fell into total admiration and humble respect for such a directed effect of spiritual grace.

There are some in the psychological field of study who would suggest that it was my injured and pain-filled psyche that solved my crisis and relived my pain; that I used the psychological "hook" of faith. All I know is that my psyche had months to work on the problems, without relief. Christ healed me in the same night that I surrendered and cried out for His help. With my pain and grief calmed upon the awakening to a new day. It was a straightforward example of, ask and it shall be given you.

So the next time the clouds of that emotional storm begin to gather, consider what happened to the disciples. Without the storm, would they have desperately sought Christ's help? Would they have had the same faith if they only traveled through tranquil seas? Or might the case be made that they were the fortunate ones to be caught out in the storm?

The Hosing

I realized it might be considered rude to make fun of, or jest, about someone's misfortunes, however, in your mother's case, I learned to make an exception. She was the mistress of distress. Your mother manage to elevated things like misfortune, injury, pain and suffering, well beyond normal human understanding. I'm convinced her destiny is to turn misery into a new art form. At the time of this writing she suffered from a sinus infection that settled into four of her teeth, her foot was in a cast from her second round of foot surgery, and she had a ruptured disc between two of her lower vertebrae.

While I tried to offer help and sympathy, she somehow coped with it all. Long ago, she came to terms with her role as Calamity Crystal. Her best hope being that she recovered from one set of traumas before the next catastrophe arrived.

Living with the magnet of malady, I tried to make certain adjustments in the way I did things. Before I fully realized that your mother had the paranormal ability to funnel disaster into her life, I wasn't that careful about what I did around her: like playing with the kids, or helping her clean house. Even something as simple as helping her go to the store could end in disaster. I learned, at your mother's expense, that any event could be a hazard to her health.

Consider the time, eight-year-old, Bobby and I ran through the house battling each other with toy guns that shot tiny plastic bullets. As the whole house was our theater of operations, we eventually moved our war into the bedroom where Crystal relaxed watching TV. As Bobby ran into the bedroom with me in hot pursuit, your mom sensed trouble.

"Don't do that in here," she blurted, "I will probably get hur..." at that instant Bobby turned and fired. Unfortunately, his hurried aim missed me and hit your mother right on the eyeball.

Think about that for a moment. Bobby and I had shot each other about a hundred-and-fifty-thousand times with the little plastic bullets bouncing off of us as if we were made of steel. But one shot, fired in the presence of your mother, seemed to take guidance from some evil telekinetic specter who directed it into the one-inch diameter of the only place it could hurt her.

Shortly after that incident, I helped her clean the kitchen. I asked her to place the upside down stools that sat on top of the counter back on the cleaned floor. Happy that her kitchen floor looked so nice, she picked up one of the stools as some perfectly timed event simultaneously distracted her. No big thing, right? Wrong. Somehow, she poked herself in the eye with the point of the stool leg.

Another time we just finished shopping and had loaded all the groceries into the trunk of the car, or so I thought.   When I nonchalantly turned and threw the trunk lid closed, the edge of the trunk lid clobbered your Mom on the top of her head. She was putting in the last package.

Your mother's special talent didn't limit itself to personal injury. She took our new boat out for an afternoon cruise and came back with the engine stuck in reverse; the eventual repair costing over $600.00. When she took my car to the mall someone tried to break into it damaging the power window. Let her drive me to the airport and on the way home she'd have a flat tire. The fact that the car was new had no influence on your mother's negative providence. The list of her misfortunes remained endless.

Another movement in her repertoire of rotten luck was that she developed allergies to insect bites. A deerfly bit her and within minutes the swelling began. She became dizzy, light headed, and breathed with difficultly. Throw a little anxiety into this brew and you have the recipe for a serious problem.

One time, we were over at Laura's, visiting and putzing in her garden. Before Crystal realized a deerfly landed on her finger, she was already bit. Immediately, the light-headed dizziness thing began and she had to sit down. Laura finished watering her garden and came over still holding the running hose. The two of us stood around your stricken mother discussing the different home remedies that had helped in the past. I suggested some Benedryl, but Laura didn't have any. Meanwhile, Crystal's condition continued to deteriorate, and she basically felt miserable. Laura and I began talking about taking her to the doctor. We also discussed how adrenaline is the body's natural defense in these kinds of situations. Both Laura and I agreed that if we could just raise your mother's adrenaline level she'd feel much better.

Laura, still holding the running hose, looked at me and asked, "So what do you want me to do?"

I paused for a moment thinking about how Crystal didn't like going to doctors. Then, with my most compassionate voice possible, I said to Laura, "Hose her down."

The look of horror on your mother's face was priceless. Apparently, just the thought of being hosed down with ice-cold water was enough, because by the time Laura and I stopped laughing, your mother felt better.

Don't get me wrong everyone has bouts of calamitous synchronicity. Here are a few of my own.

F. Edward Marx   To Mandi, with Love

The Do's and Mostly Don'ts of Do-It-Yourselfing

Sometime during my adolescence, I developed the attitude that there wasn't anything I couldn't do myself. I think it all started when I put on my own socks. By the time I turned sixteen and bought my first car, I was hopelessly ensnarled in self-confidence. I didn't realize that it was all over but the crying—and the first-aid.

In my youth doing-it-yourself was not some casual decision made while leisurely sipping my morning coffee. Doing it myself originated in what I came to learn in business as a temporary cash flow problem. This meant that if I couldn't flow some cash, I had to fix it myself. Usually, to the astonishment of those around me, including myself, I succeeded. Not to mention adding critical automotive components like a new eight-track tape deck with approximately 10,000 watts of power, six or seven speakers, and a reverberator. What my "system" lack in acoustical clarity, it certainly made up for in volume. And if you liked listening to a rock concert at the bottom of the Grand Canyon, you'd think you died and gone to heaven.

Even today, I will occasionally find myself in a temporary cash flow situation. So instead of calling in a repair team that charges by the half-second, I will at least take a crack at trying to fix it myself. I'm also convinced that when the fates governing my life feel they need a good laugh, they conjure just the right circumstances to get the most mileage out of setting me up.

For instance, consider the time I bought the pontoon boat. On the second day we owned it, your mother Calamity Crystal took the boat out and returned home towed by another boat. As I tied the boat up to the dock all she could do was shrug her shoulders while offering the explanation that the engine got stuck in reverse. Of course, she

- 16 -

didn't realize that the fates had cleverly crafted the fact that I spent every available penny buying the boat. This, of course, meant that I would have to try to fix it myself. I gathered my tools as the muses gathered their soft drinks and popcorn.

To gain access to the engine, I had to lift the engine compartment hatch covered by a long, cushioned sun deck. Unfastening the latches, I raised the sun deck to inspect the engine. Unable to find anything wrong, I lowered the sun deck and decided to start the engine to see if I could force the gearshift mechanism out of its stuck position. A few moments later, the boat and I were in the channel in front of the house doing backward loops. Concentrating my attention on working the gearshift loose, I just happened to look over my shoulder in time to notice that I was on a collision course with the neighbor's dock.

Trying not to think about the on rushing wreck or how I would explain to my neighbor that he didn't really need that long of a dock, I turned the engine off. Fortunately, this added about two more seconds to my estimated time of arrival. I'm still not sure if it was inspiration or insanity, but I poised myself to leap over the sun deck and land on the dock. My plan was to get to the dock ahead of the boat then push back to lessen the impact. Upon arriving at what I considered my maximum leaping range, I grabbed the railing on the back of the sun deck and hurled myself off into space.

Well, guess what?

I forgot to latch the sun deck down when I inspected the engine. Instead of going up, over and on to the neighbors dock, I went up, the sun deck flipped open, and I careened head-over-heels into the lake. While I'm underwater waiting for my head to be crushed between the dock and the left pontoon, the fates not wanting me to actually suffer serious injury, perform one of their minor miracles. Somehow, my head ended up in the gap between the shut off engine and the pontoon. Since it was shallow enough to stand up, I popped out of the water and did my best Hercules imitation. I'm not sure how, but I managed to stop the boat before it crashed into the dock.

Upon my return to our dock with the sun deck hanging by its broken hinges, your mother awaited my arrival. While holding her sides and squeezing her legs together to counteract the effect the lake weeds hanging from my head had on her bladder, she tried to catch her breath. Finally, she blurted out, "Are you all right? He-he, I told the kids not to laugh, ha-ha, until we were sure you were all right, he-he. But when we saw you pop out of the water, ha-ha, we couldn't help ourselves, he-he. Are you, okay?"

Another time the fates felt that they needed some entertainment was right after I bought the lake-house. Before moving in, I wanted to do some remolding. The main job was to take out the wall separating the kitchen from the living room. Once the wall was removed, I needed to install a support beam that spanned the length of the torn out wall. The recommended material was two thick Microlam boards placed side by side to create a 14-foot beam that would support the span of the missing wall.

Working by myself, I propped the first beam in place with a two-by-four brace. As I lifted the second beam into position next to the first one, I bumped the two-by-four. The no-longer-suspended-beam crashed down, glancing off the side of my head and clipping my ear like the edge of a ninety-pound guillotine. As my knees buckled from the blow to my noggin, I realized I still held the other beam over my head. Which if I let go would finish the job the first beam had intended.

After setting the beam down, I began looking around the floor for my ear--which I was sure had been sheared off. Not seeing it anywhere at my feet, I gingerly touch the side of my head to see just how many strands of flesh were still holding my dangling ear. Upon careful tactile inspection, I realized that my ear was still attached even though I had no feeling, other than excruciating pain.

It was like the specter of construction accidents came down and went "BAP" right on the side of my head, providing me with the reminder, "DON'T BE STUPID."

F. Edward Marx   To Mandi, with Love

I'm not sure if it was my semi-conscious state due the blow to my head, but I could swear that somewhere off in the distance I heard the fates laughing, "Ha Ha Ha, I wonder if he will ever learn."

Rooms of the Heart

Mandi memories and feelings are created each moment of life, however, the largest percentage come from our interactions with others. If we're willing to explore our inner self, we can discover those chambers were emotions live. They are called by many names: love, hate, frustration, or desire, just to name a few, and I have found that just about any deep feeling seems to create a psychological space all its own.

For instance, consider the intense emotion filled room of passion and desire—that feeling of falling in love. No one person can enter that realm by his or her self. It takes a special combined chemistry. Someone else must offer just the right key to unlock the door that lets us in. Then, the ignited sparks fly and the butterflies flutter. Ironically, even though those feelings are contained in your own heart, you cannot enter unless someone else provides the key. Unfortunately, I feel it necessary to offer this warning. If you're not careful, you can become consumed by the single-minded anticipation of when you can return to that special place. And some people will do almost anything to be able to return.

We all love the feeling of falling in love. Consequently, some people go from one relationship to another looking for that special person who holds their particular key. Unfortunately, this can lead to a series of deteriorating relationships as the person tries to force open the door to that special joy filled room. It's difficult to accept that you can never again enter into those special emotions once they have been closed, and the deep sense of loss that is felt when we lose someone we love is not just the loss of their physical presence, it is also the sense of being locked out of the future. To live life knowing of such a place but not being able to go there is a huge pain in the heart. But sometimes you have to do just that—live life with the pain. Because without that special person you are locked out of that place that only they could open.

I find it so ironic that those we truly love end up hurting us the most. Whether they leave us for another or they die, the intensity of that hurt would never have been felt for someone we cared little for. However, in their passing, those we love can still open other doors and show each of us new emotions that are part of the human experience. If we have the fortitude to enter into those difficult places, we can gain strength and understanding that we would otherwise never know.

While it may seem a burden that others hold these keys, consider it fortunate to have known such love. Some people live their whole life never experiencing the adventure of Eros. The important lesson here is to remember that others can and do open you to the emotions of life. Some will come along and try to open the doors of resentment, anger, or revenge. Others will try to get you to enter into areas that they can control or manipulate, but each of us has the choice of whether or not to enter in.

When someone tries to turn the keys to anger or frustration, you can stand on the threshold of that opening and make a conscious decision not to go there. It helps to create a mental picture of that door and form a visualization of yourself standing on the threshold. Then, slam that emotion shut. Take an inventory of how you feel and see if there are any other doors leading to negative emotions that need closing and slam them shut as well. Possibly, while you're taking this self-examination you may find a door that leads to understanding or compassion. Work out why this person affects you in this way. Ask yourself if there is a lesson here. Maybe, by entering into those positive feelings, you can offer the key that opens a door for the person trying to control or anger you. You never know, you just might provide a new dimension to someone else's well being.

I had to learn of the rooms of the heart the hard way. I left a wake of destruction before I finally understood that I couldn't force those old doors open. Revelation 3:6 explains that what door God closes no one can open, and what door He opens no one can close.

F. Edward Marx   To Mandi, with Love

Now its time to get on with life and see what other doors destiny has waiting.

The Improper Care and Feeding of a Best Friend

I first met Mac during summer vacation of fourth grade. Having just moved into the neighborhood, I was the proverbial new kid on the block. As I wandered around getting the "feel" for things, I noticed Mac sitting on his porch with a magnifying glass.

I yelled, "Hey, what'ca doin?"

"I'm burning ants."

"Cool! Can I try it?"

"Sure."

To the dismay of many an ant colony we have been best friends ever since.

As with any insect eradicating kids worthy of the title "bug-killers" we soon graduated from the effective but slow process of focusing our pin-point of light and eliminating one ant at a time, to the mass extermination of chemical warfare. Using the stored ingredients in our parent's garages, we concocted some very creative, if not always effective potions, with the main ingredient usually something flammable.

Satisfied with the volatility of our recipe, we poured down the ant hole a witches brew of gasoline, motor oil, turpentine, pesticide and anything else that might burn or explode. Then, we'd trail a liquid fuse off to one side, light it, and take several quick steps backwards. Sometimes the mini volcano that erupted wasn't all that small. How we manage to avoid burning down the garage, I'll never know.

Somehow, Mac always seemed to get the blunt end of our friendship. Actually it was more like the sharp end. One of us had seen an old Viking movie where two opposing warriors stood next to big wooden posts and threw axes at each other's post as a test of manhood. Since we didn't have posts and axes at our disposal (thank

God), we improvised. After pacing off a respectable distance we bravely faced each other with darts in hand. Then, on the count of three, we threw our darts at the cardboard boxes next to our legs. Mac's dart landed squarely in the middle of my box; my dart landed squarely in the middle of his leg.

Not long after he stopped limping from our test of manhood, we rode double on my bike. Mac clung valiantly to the handlebars with his feet on top of my front fender. As we thumped down the curb of a busy street, Mac's foot slipped off the front fender and got wedge between the spinning spokes and steel fork that held the wheel on. As we were traveling at a fairly high rate of speed his foot did quite a bit of damage to my front wheel. After extracting his mangled flesh and shredded shoe from my wheel assembly, I wobbled back to his house at warp speed. Standing in front of his mother, panting hard, yet calmly, I explained, "Mrs. Peters, I'm not sure how it happened, but Mac hurt his foot pretty bad. I think you'd better come with me and get him."

As Mac hobbled to the car, his foot already the size of a cantaloupe, not to mention alternately flashing the colors of the rainbow, he held up his shredded footgear and said, "Look what happened to my shoe."

Weeks later, we continued showing off his sneaker. Telling the story of how he hurt his foot, and proudly pointing to the dried up skin still hanging from the spokes of my front wheel.

In high school, Mac had a crush on one of our senior-class beauty queens. Frustrated that he couldn't quite capture her attention, he decided to take it to the next level. Of course, as teenagers we didn't know that the next level after frustration was…desperation.

One Friday night, as we sat drinking our almost legal six packs of beer. Mac lamented about his romantic woes and the lack of feminine attention. One of our psychologically advanced (his father was a doctor so he thought he could help buddies) came up with this idea. He suggested that Mac needed a way to gain her sympathy. His personal psycho-theory being that if Mac could exhibit enough suffering she would surely give him the attention he needed to begin the romance. The question then became, what could Mac do to show he visibly needed comforting the next time he met her face to face? We bantered about cuts, bruises, and broken bones, all of which seem too severe for the task at hand.

"How about a black eye," someone suggested.

Mac thought about it for a few moments.

We talked about how black eyes, while *almost* painless, were an excellent origin for sympathy, as well as a masculine badge of honor. Mac tilted his beer back, emptied it and said, "Yeah, that'll do it."

So, my Rhodes scholar buddies and I implemented a plan to "help" him. The intricacies of our scheme consisted of Mac standing next to the bed and one of us socking him in the eye. Then, as he fell backward on to the mattress, voi-la, a black eye.

There was only one small detail left to work out, who would put a fist in our buddy Mac's eye?

Of course, as his best friend, the task of helping Mac win his true love fell upon yours truly.

With great fan fare, and the anesthetic achieved by shooting a couple of beers, Mac lined himself up with the bed and offered this final instruction: "You better make sure you hit me hard enough, I don't want to have to do this again."

I'm not exactly sure what went wrong with our plan as Mac ended up with a splendid shiner. Unfortunately, the object of his desire was not impressed, and he had to eventually come to grips with the fact that she just wasn't worth all the trouble.

Sometime after completing our mandatory internment called High School. Mac and I decided to go out West hunting, fishing, and living off the land. We loaded up my car and sometime around the end of August we bid "Adios" to our less than enthusiastic parents. We didn't have a lot of money so living off the land was actually a necessity.   By about the fourth week, our meager supplies were running low, so we decide we'd better get to a spot where the fish were plentiful and easy to catch.

After setting up camp, we slid into our hip-boots and began to wade out to where we saw the trout rising to eat the bugs on the water. The problem was that the trout were out deeper than our hip boots were tall. Our only available solution was to hop from one submerged rock to another. This clever tactic kept the water line below our boots while getting us out far enough to reach the fish. There is only one small problem with this style of fishing, those rocks can be really slippery. I'm not sure how many times I watched Mac's footing slip landing him butt first in the ice-cold water. Then, as the submerged rock momentarily halted his plunge, he'd flail his arms madly about in search of a non-existence handhold until he slowly sank out of sight.

Just when I'd think he was gone forever, he'd porpoise high above the surface flinging iridescent water droplets into the crisp mountain air. It was difficult to understand him at such moments, but I thought I heard him screaming about how he'd never fish again and if he had to eat another fish for breakfast he would rather just shoot himself. Of course, he was just kidding. He would eat another fish for breakfast, and for lunch, and for dinner.

We manage to choke down hard biscuits and fish three meals a day for about a week, but the realization formed that we'd have to resort to desperate measures—we contemplated getting jobs. We talked about picking apples or working for a rancher. Fortunately, good judgment eventually prevailed, and Mac decided to call home for money instead. We cleaned up by taking a bath in an autumn mountain stream--it's amazing how fast you can get clean in 50-degree water.

After breaking camp we headed down the mountain for our monthly trip into town. Since Mac's money gram wouldn't arrive until the next day, we spent the night just outside of town overlooking a magnificent canyon. Mac slept in the front seat with the steering wheel for company as I curled up in back. Had we not been destitute and starving, watching the sun set over such beautiful landscape might have been a pleasant experience.

Restocked with supplies and a little money left over for necessities like beer. We headed back into the mountains, this time to go Mule deer hunting high up on a mountain plateau as far away from fish as we could get. Unfortunately, we were as far away from Mule deer as we could get as well. We climbed mountains and ridges. We hiked up the steepest of trails and tiptoed the narrowest of ridges, but we never saw hide nor hair of a deer. In fact, Mac became so good at climbing he started experimenting with new ways to get down. His most expedient method turned out to be slipping on some loose shale. Then, he fell over an edge and landed about 15 feet below. Not yet satisfied with the results of his experiment, and with still a lot of mountain left, he rolled off that ledge, landed on his rifle strapped to his back, gasped for air, and slid another hundred yards through loose rocks and small prickly cactus. Eventually, he intersected with a large boulder that ended his experiment.

After about three weeks of hiking, climbing, and falling off mountains, we hadn't seen a single Muley. Once again we faced a single item menu. This time it was chili. We had made a huge pot of Mountain Chili. The reason we called it Mountain Chili was because after the third day it had accumulated mountain leaves, mountain bugs, mountain twigs, mountain pebbles, and mountain green stuff. We never intended to keep eating the chili as our steak-fest was only a rifle shot away, but that rifle shot never came. So, whenever we got really hungry we slid the chili over a foot or two onto the fire. Even though chili is one of those dishes that gets better with age, I've never heard anyone say, "You know this chili is better this week than it was all of last week."

In our wildest imaginings we never thought we'd see this moment, but after the fourth or fifth straight day of breakfast, lunch, and dinner chili we were yearning for some crispy pan-fried trout.

Elk Hunting

Mac Peters and I had been up in the western Colorado Rockies for about three weeks hunting mule deer. We camped in the wilderness and lived off the land. Which is another way of saying we starved, and froze whatever appendage that had the misfortune to stick out of our sleeping bags.

As Mac stoked the morning fire to life-giving warmth, he tried to break through the layer of ice that formed on our pot of mountain chili. I couldn't help noticing him inspecting the frozen chunks to see what new ingredients might have taken up residence during the night. Satisfied that nothing unusual had crept in, just the bugs, twigs, leaves, and green stuff that we'd grown accustomed to, he looked at me with a sad forlorn expression. Finally, he lamented, "I really don't think I can eat any more chili."

"Yeah, I know, neither can I. I really thought we would have some nice venison steaks by now."

"What do you want to do? We don't have any money."

"I know," I replied. "I guess we'll just have to resort to drastic measures. I hate to even think about it, but there is really only one thing left that we can do."

"I called home for money last time, it's your turn."

I knew Mac consider this minor point to be important, and since the alternative was more chili, I gave into his adolescent logic. "Okay, let's break camp, get cleaned up, and I'll call home when we get to town."

Breaking camp was simple enough. It's removing the layer of "camp" that one's body acquires after three weeks in the late autumn bush that is the real chore.

We separated our least dirty pants and shirt from the wad of clothing growing in the corner of the tent, shook them, beat them, and hung them in the breeze. Then armed with a bar of soap and a towel, we did the hardest thing one can do in the October Rockies. We jumped into four feet of cryogenic fluid called a mountain stream. Nineteen-seconds later we were clean, shaved, our hair washed, and teeth brushed.

"You ready?"

"Yep!"

Since my folks hadn't heard from me for about six-weeks, I figured a friendly little call to let them know I was all right along with an: "Oh, by the way, could you send us five-hundred-dollars," might just work.

Later that afternoon we picked up our check from Western Union, and after three weeks of mountain solitude, we headed for the nearest bar.

Both Mac and I were the kind of characters that you could throw into a room full of strangers and a few smiles later, not to mention a couple of rounds for the bar, we'd have a dozen new friends. It wasn't long in The Do Drop Inn before we knew the owner, his daughter, Marshal, Bill, Wild Bill, Big John, and Crazy Leonard. Thirty beers later and we had Big John, Crazy Leonard, and Wild Bill in tears about our three weeks of invisible Mule deer hunting with Bill and Marshal telling us, we should have come with them as they got two each.

The next day Mac and I were walking the outskirts of town when an old pickup pulled along side. Big John stuck a wide snaggle-tooth grin out the window and said, "Hop in the back, we'll give you a lift."

We cruised along enjoying the Rocky Mountain sunshine and blue sky when Wild Bill decided to be hospitable. He opened a fifth of whiskey took a Texas swig then passed it to Big John who drove. Big John took a gulp, stuck the fifth out the window and handed it to Mac. Pickup truck etiquette required Mac to take an obligatory gulp. Then, of course, it was my turn. I downed the firewater and passed it through the passenger side window back to Wild Bill. This all took place in the days prior to understanding the consequences of drunk driving with the four of us merrily traveling along passing the time of day, along with the whiskey.   As a seemingly minor afterthought, Big John stuck his head out of the window and yelled, "If the cops pull us over, you better make a run for it."

"How come?" Mac hollered back.

"Cuz, this truck is stolen, ha-ha-ha."

I looked through the back window at Wild Bill who was also laughing and nodding his head in agreement with this latest tidbit of humorous information.

Fortunately for Mac and I, rural Colorado did not have an abundance of police officers. Even though we were only nineteen at the time, and Wild Bill and Big John seemed like a lot of fun, we never spent any more time with them after that. We did however, go back to the Do Drop Inn and hung around with Marshal and Bill.

Those two were quite a pair. Four years older than Mac and I, Bill and Marshal along with their life long buddy Mike had enlisted for a tour of duty in Vietnam. The three of them left as idealistic young men hoping to change the world and enforce the American dream on to other cultures. Sadly only two of them returned. Disillusioned, shot at, ambushed, and booby-trapped, they had acquired the give-a-shit attitude that young men get after passing the annihilation test.

They seemed to have mastered two concepts while in Vietnam. One was, if bullets aren't whizzing by you, how bad can it be? And what are they going to do, they can't send me back to Vietnam.

We found new friends in Bill and Marshal, with Marshal inviting us to camp out in his living room until opening day of Elk season. At which time he promised to take us with him: "To a place where the elk are so thick that if you aren't careful you'll get trampled!"

The day before elk season, we arrived at a mountain clearing to set up camp. Bill dropped the tailgate of his pickup, pulled out his cooler, popped open a beer, and announced to the world, "Home sweet home."

F. Edward Marx   To Mandi, with Love

Apparently that was the extent of his set up activities. Mac and I, on the other hand, had to pitch our tent, set up a campfire, and figure out how we were going to stay warm for the next week or so.

Needless-to-say, a tent in the October Rockies is not the coziest place in the Western hemisphere. Mac and I got fully dressed each night to go to bed. Then, tucked deep within our goose down bags we slept warm and dry. The problem was getting up in the morning. The temperature dropped to somewhere around zero during the night, and in case we forgot how cold it really was, ice crystals from our overnight breathing formed an iridescent reminder on the inside of the tent's walls.

Sometime during the past September, we learned that ice-cold boots were a form of torture that should be outlawed by the Geneva Convention. As uncomfortable as it might seem, we slept curled up with our boots. I'm convinced that if there is ever another Inquisition, the only measure that need be adopted to make some poor soul convert would be to force them to strap on a pair of boots that spent the night out in the Rockies.

The real trick was not to be the first one up in the morning needing to take a leak. Because whoever got up first spent the next twenty or thirty minutes building the fire. But once you heard flames crackling and smelled the coffee, getting up and putting on warm boots to stroll over to the fire wasn't so bad.

Opening day of Elk season arrived with each of us setting off into the rugged terrain. Directed by the map that Marshall had drawn in the snow the day before, I found myself struggling through the pre-dawn woods. Not seeing a single landmark to match Marshal's chicken scratches in the snow, I stumbled into a small clearing. Stopping to rest and gain my bearings, I relished in the morning sun as it broke over the winter mountains.

The noise began as a low rumble. Then as the sound closed in on me, the tumult amplified to the point that I thought a herd of elephants were charging through the woods.

Small trees snapped in half.

Hooves pounded the earth.

Breaking twigs and branches crackled closer and closer as I lifted my rifle. Steadying the sights against the tree that I hid behind, my heart began to pound. This was the big moment I had waited for. Mac and I had endured months of misery and spent all of our money in anticipation of this incredible event. With my gun raised and level, I was about to come face to face with one of the most magnificent creatures on this planet.

It's hard to explain the amount of adrenalin that is released by the approach of big game. I suspect it goes back to some prehistoric collective memory when the hunter was never sure if he was going to get supper or be supper. I tried to choke my zeppelin-sized heart down to where it belonged, but each chest-pounding beat gave me the distinct impression that it was trying to dislodge itself from my ribcage. Instantly, eight to ten cow-elk appeared and stopped dead in their tracks about forty-feet in front of me.

Huddled tightly together, they knew I was close. With their noses pointed straight up in the air, they tried to locate my aromatic origins. Suddenly, a huge bull-elk ran right into the middle of the herd. Sensing my presence, the cows gathered around the bull placing themselves between him and danger. A very effective tactic I might add.

While I'm trying to get a clear shot, the elk with their own agenda, decided upon another plan. Still not knowing where I hid, they just stampeded straight ahead. Had it not been for the tree I stood behind they would have run right over me. While those massive animals bulldozed by at arms length, I had this hallucinatory image of myself lying on the ground trampled flat like a cartoon character with my two eyes bugging out, and Mac standing over me asking, "What happened?" Then, out of my flattened carcass, I grunted the word, "Elk!"

I snapped back to reality as that magnificent bull, his antlers resembling a small oak tree, passed close enough that I could see his nostrils flaring and smell his elk breath.

Moments later, dejected, realizing I've missed the chance of a lifetime, I laid my rifle across a stump to kneel down to get a good looks at the empty elk tracks. Placing my finger tips reverently into the large hoof prints, I assured myself that, yes, a herd of elk just thundered by. While I'm bent over, scratching my head and wondering how I could be so unfortunate, a bigger bull materialized. He was following the herd that just tried to trample me. As he charged past me, I had just enough time to get a really good look at him, and my rifle lying on the log a few feet away. Mesmerized by his stature, and the rack that looked twice the size of the giant that just disappeared, I could do nothing but watch as he galloped by.

There is really only one way to handle such a situation. You calmly sit down, look up at the clear morning sky, and throw a fit. Of, course, while you're throwing the fit, it's important to remind yourself, at least a thousand times, that you saw two trophy elk, and never fired a shot. That you spent the last two months starving, fighting off the frigid cold, and bathing in frozen streams for a opportunity to hunt just such an animal, only to miss your chance…twice. Then, you get up out of the shallow ditch that your writhing body created, shake off the dirt and leaves, and try to convince yourself that there are more fish in the sea, or in this case, Elk on the mountain.

That night, back at camp everyone's retelling the day's adventures. Marshal finally got around to asking me, "What happened to you? I told you to go left at that fallen log then half way up the draw make a right on the game trail and meet me at the top of the ridge. I'll bet you didn't see any elk at all, did ya?"

"No, I saw some elk."

"Oh, just cows, huh, no bulls?"

"No, I saw some bulls."

Some bulls? You mean more than one!"

"Yeah."

"You didn't shoot?"

"No."

"Why not?"

"Remember when you said that if you weren't careful the elk would run you right over."

"Yeah!"

"Well…"

Consequences

Mandi, do you ever think of consequences?

As you get older and your responsibilities grow, so does the weight of the your actions.

As a reasonably bright man, I've asked myself a thousand times: Why didn't I perceive the effect my actions would have on others?

I realize now it was for three main reasons: one, I didn't want to. I allowed my selfishness to overshadow and even dominate my conscience. I wanted a taste of the forbidden fruit, and just as Adam failed to listen to his spirit or conscience, I too gave into the desires of this world.

Then after desires is conceived, it gives birth to sin, and sin when it is full grown gives birth to death. James 1:15

The second reason turned out to be that I resented feeling like I had been trapped. Resentment is an incredibly devious and powerful human failing resulting in bitterness. Bitterness is an emotional toxin that poisons the container that holds it, and it's never long before it begins to spill over.

The third reason was that my arrogance had grown to the point where I felt there wasn't any situation that I couldn't control, or anyone I couldn't manipulate.

Each of those things is a foul stench to the senses of God, and I can hardly imagine what aroma is achieved when they are all combined. For the sake of my eternal soul I needed His discipline.

Now His chastisement is one of the most sacred things in my life. I have learned that a Father who loves, disciplines, and a son or daughter who loves, learns from His wisdom.

I chose to ignore the consequences that were so easily predicted. While I would never dream of hurting the people that I loved, I did exactly that. Somewhere in the midst of daily living I misplaced my conscience, or deliberately set it aside. Once that happened, I lost my connection to God, and I've learned that, that is a consequence of extreme significance. For without that connection, we are no different than the beasts of the field, acting on biology or instinct, or something even worse—evil itself.

It's all about how we approach the future. You have a choice. You can proceed blindly forward, or you can chose to think about the consequences.

Webster defines consequences as (1) a conclusion derived through logic; (2) something produced by a cause or necessarily following from a set of conditions; (3) importance with respect to power to produce an effect.

For me, those definitions do not take the meaning of consequence quite far enough. The true understanding of consequences will provide one with the ability to comprehend and even "see" the future.

When one is dealing with the natural laws, the ability to predict the future becomes almost second nature. If you drop an egg, gravity will pull it to the floor. The ability to predict the consequence of a broken egg is almost a certainty. But when it comes to human nature the ability to predict the future with any certainty is difficult to say the least.

Since consequences are based on present activities the key to tomorrow can be found in what we do today. And even more importantly, if we neglect our spirituality and ignore God's laws the consequences are disaster. What many people don't realize is that sin is the legal access through which satan enters our lives. Sin has consequences.

God didn't give us His laws to bind or restrict personal activity. He gave us His laws in order to limit the spread of pain and anguish from the exercising of immature freewill.

Wrong choices equate to suffering, tears, and turmoil. Obedience to God results in peace, trust, and understanding. God is

Love. There can only be one outcome when we make Him our goal. He is the author and finisher of our very essence if we allow it of Him.

In addition to God's laws we possess conscience and memory. With each providing us the opportunity to rationalize the present circumstances in order to determine a high probability outcome.

When confronted with a set of circumstances or problems, the ability to apply reason often provides a clear understanding of what will happen next. This offers a choice of actions--when we choose to pay attention.

Our past provides us with a library of experience-based consequences to draw upon: when I did this, this problem occurred, or when I said that, those feelings were the results. By paying attention to the cause and effect of daily life there comes a time when similar circumstances will repeat. By recalling the previous consequences we will know the resultant future. And if God's law prohibits a certain activity, I can guarantee that someone will suffer from that course of action.

Thinking about the consequences and then selecting a specific option offers the opportunity to enhance a future pleasant experience or decrease/eliminate the effects of an approaching problem.   However, this only works in combination with the conscience. Exclude that and the same mistakes will be repeated over and over, even when the painful outcome is clearly known.

In the jumble of daily life we are all faced with a thousand decisions. By filtering those decisions through a spiritually based awareness, we will invariably make the best decision possible. However, a hasty decision made without conscience and little thought about what happens next will cause us, and/or those around us, more problems.

The future is created by our thoughts and actions with each having a consequence. Understand that, and you will know the future.

The next story is about unconsidered consequences. My friends and I were very lucky.

- 37 -

F. Edward Marx   To Mandi, with Love

Riding the Wind (Shield)

At seventeen years old it took some major begging to finally get my father's approval to use my car for a camping trip with three of my buddies. The necessary intensity of my pleading wasn't because my Dad was so strict or over bearing it was more because he too was once 17. Eventually, he managed to quell all of his premonitions of disaster, and with great reluctance, agreed to the trip.

Bright and early, Mac, Phil, Luke, and I loaded my car, climbed in and eagerly began our adventure. As I backed out of Luke's driveway, I looked over my shoulder and said, "Here we go!" Only to bang into the Oak tree next to Luke house.

Of course, Phil, Luke and Mac thought this incredibly funny. I on the other hand did not. The softball size dent in my "Cherry" 65 Mustang provided me an indelible lesson in the value of never using your own vehicle for any type of "adventure"-- especially one with friends. I think Shakespeare put it best, "Experience is the best teacher, but it is a fool who has no other."

Except for four teenagers singing rock-and-roll at the top of their lungs for a hundred miles, the trip was uneventful. We arrived in the general vicinity of our destination, with the growing concern of how we could procure the main staple of our needed provisions—beer. Since none of us were old enough to buy alcohol we had a slight logistical problem to overcome.

Due to some undemocratic consensus that I looked the oldest, they elected me to go into the first party store we came upon. Disguising myself as an adult by donning a pair of sunglasses, I sallied forth into the unknown.

Inside the store, I placed a six-pack and a bottle of wine on the counter. The clerk smiled and asked, "Will there be anything else?"

"Ahhhh…yes! Two cold cases of beer from the cooler, please."

- 38 -

F. Edward Marx   To Mandi, with Love

As I walked around the corner of the parking lot carrying the two cases of brewskies, the three stooges saw me. By the display of their exhilaration, anyone else would have thought they were in the midst of a brawl, but I knew they were striking each other with frolicking punches of happiness, and throwing headlocks of joy.

Having enough sense to know that society wasn't quite ready for us, we picked a secluded spot near the lake where no one else camped. That afternoon a couple of unwitting campers set up in our proximity. They didn't realize they were about to be kept awake until 4:00am by beer infected teenagers. Needless to say, the next day when we got up around noon the other campers were no longer present. Apparently, their style of camping differed somewhat from ours.

While the planned duration for this trip was a week, by the middle of the afternoon of the first day we were bored.   Luke mentioned hiking, or bird watching by a babbling brook, but the empty beer cans that pelted him helped him reconsider his suggestion

Northern woods are serene and beautiful, but they are not chockfull of things that teenage boys like to do--mainly because they are not chockfull with teenage girls. While cruising around hanging out of the windows of my Mustang, someone came up with the idea that it might be more fun to ride outside rather than inside.

Luke and Phil climbed onto the hood, sitting with their backs against the windshield. I stuck my head out of the driver's side window, Casey Jones style, as we recklessly rode around the old seldom-used back roads. While Phil and Luke clung desperately to my windshield wipers screaming for me to slow down, Mac and I laughed hysterically. I would have gone faster except for my concern for the wipers. Since I had no idea what the maximum passenger rating of a windshield wiper was, I felt I should remain at a conservative thirty-five to forty-miles-per-hour

After several miles of Mac and I having a really good time, I stopped.   Of course, Phil and Luke wanted us to share in the excitement and decided it was our turn to "ride the wind." Showing just how ignorant teenage boys can be, we exchanged places.

Not to be out done by the good time Mac and I had at their expense, Phil took off like a bat out of hell. This upset me slightly as Phil obviously showed no concern what-so-ever for the safety and well being of my windshield wipers. In the mean time, Mac and I screamed every four-letter superlative in our vocabulary trying to get him to slow down. Unfortunately, this only seemed to make Phil and Luke laugh twice as hard--probably because we were going twice as fast.

Phil was having such a good time that we might still be pinned to the windshield had it not been for the highway that my Mustang, hurtling forward at about seventy, with two lunatics on the hood, suddenly crossed. Had another car been innocently traveling along on this major thoroughfare our little bit of fun would have been a huge tragedy.

Phil stopped my car as we all looked at each other realizing just how lucky we'd been. We quietly drove back to camp with projections of what our foolishness could have caused, never again to ride the windshield.

Miss Bliss and the Lesson for the Future

Mandi, I can't help wondering how you are doing. Because of the damage to your voice, you have always felt different than the rest of the group. Personally, to me, your difference made you that much more endearing. But I know you've had to struggle with it. To go through childhood different than the rest is a problem. But someday you will realize that what makes you different is a gift, and that there is a purpose to everything under heaven. The adversities that you've overcome in life have advanced you in ways that you are yet to understand, but someday you will be able to tap into what makes you so special, and there will be no goal that you cannot achieve. In the meantime work hard on your education; it is the foundation for the rest of your life. This next story is an example.

* * *

Making your own luck is a simple idea with profound intricacies that weave and influence our entire lives. An example of this was when I took typing as an elective class during my senior year. I didn't take that class in order to be the first Captain of the football team in the history of my high school to take typing. I really enrolled in Miss Bliss's class in order to be with my girl friend. Had I known that Miss Bliss took teaching typing seriously, I would never have consider her class--true love or not.

Miss Bliss was about 5 feet 1, and shrinking. With a long pointy nose that supported her reading spectacles, she ruled the domain of her class room with a wrinkled face, an iron will, and last but not least, a wooden ruler.

While she roamed the entire classroom, her favorite station was to hover over me, ruler at the ready. Then, on some horrendous mistake on my part, like not typing the correct letter with my little

Pinkie finger, she'd rap me on the knuckles with the edge of the Wooden Maiden and offer advise like: "If your in my class Mister, you are going to learn to type correctly."

The reason she used the edge was due to the time she hit me hard enough with her old ruler, the one responsible for battering a thousand pinkies' before mine, that it broke in half.

Apparently that ruler was some kind of classroom heirloom bestowed on her by Socrates. Because the look of wrinkled astonishment followed by her steely-eyed expression let me know in no uncertain terms that I was responsible for not only terminating an item that enjoyed the most favored tool status, but that I had also broken off an extension of her psyche. A portion that probably had more personality then she did.

The mere breaking of a museum artifact was bad enough, but when the whole class started laughing, which of course made her madder, I knew I was doomed. Fortunately, due to the injury to Miss Bliss's psyche the remainder of that class was very quite. Not a single pinkie got whacked, nor a single "YELP" of pain heard. It was almost like Miss Bliss was no longer there. Relief flooded over me when the bell finally rang ending the torture of that surreal time.

The very next day, Miss Bliss returned carrying the mother-of-all-rulers. It was thick, boldly printed and had the look of an industrial strength beam. Without hesitation she loomed over me waiting for the opportunity to try out her new teaching aid. Relishing in the undisciplined movement of my untrained pinkies, she expertly connected with a knuckle, at the same time cocking her ear slightly to fully absorb the new sound of hard wood thwacking against my tender flesh and bone.

Pleased with her new form of entertainment, she seemed quite satisfied with the walloping to my poor little pinkie.

After about a month of some seriously sore fingers, I typed correctly. And by the end of the school year, I actually achieved the lofty goal of a "C" average.

Considering that when I went to high school there was not even an inkling of computers, faxes, E-Mail or the Internet, upon graduation of Miss Bliss's class, I knew that as long as I lived I'd never touch a keyboard again.

Thirty years later, I spend hours a day on the keyboard. Those previously deemed to be unneeded, yet hard earned typing skills offer me a proficient interface to the electronic world. As I look back through the crystal clarity of hindsight, I now consider that wrinkled little old lady one of the best teachers I ever had, appreciating the gift that she gave me on a daily basis.

Today, I consider the completion of Miss Bliss's typing class one of those accidental strokes of luck that the Wooden Maiden and I made happen.

Making your own luck is a reflection of your past, in that you reap what you sow. Someone defined luck as preparedness meeting opportunity. Hard work and a positive attitude will create an aura of opportunity. By being conscientiousness, and putting in that extra effort often translates into being selected when some special circumstances occur. Strive to learn as much in school or apprenticeship as possible, then years later, opportunities to use what you have learned will move you ever closer to your true potential.

F. Edward Marx   To Mandi, with Love

Forgiveness

Mandi, mistakes change lives. I had to learn that lesson the hard way, and words will never express the depth of my sorrow. But all of that is in the past, and as difficult as it maybe to accomplish, the past should not be dwelt upon. Christ told us: *No one who puts his hand to the plow and looks back is fit for service in the kingdom of God.*

This means that we should neither be judgmental of others, nor should we carry the bitterness that life is so good at heaping upon us. Once you begin to seek your divine nature, putting your hands on the plow so to speak, you must not look back. That is because the goal of living within your divine destiny can only be found by looking forward—by being Spirit led. And if you take your eye off that target, even for a moment, you will become distracted, unable to plow a straight and proper furrow.

Christ also made it clear that if God can forgive you and I for our mountain of offenses, that it is our spiritual duty to forgive those who have offended us. He told us that when God forgives, He puts our sins as far from Him as the East is from the West. That, of course, is a metaphor for two things that can never come together

Remember that the present is what really matters. Unfortunately, as long as a person lives in a world of bitterness, brought about by the past, he or she will remain separated from God and the divine destiny He has planned.

Rage, fury, hatred, and unforgiveness are characteristics of the enslaver. Show me someone living in bitterness, and I will show you a person immersed in pain and existing in a windowless dungeon of stifled emotions that blocks out the light of understanding and peace.

Show me hate, and I'll show you injury and suffering.

Show me unforgiveness, and I'll show you unholy chains that bind that person to the past that they so desperately want to forget.

Love, Truth, and Forgiveness are the only weapons that will combat satan, and the evil he unleashes through the spiritual doorway that an offense to another person opens.

Forgiveness defies logic. The nature of the ego is to hold onto resentment, which only reinforces the original pain: a kind of psychological insulation that an injured ego erroneously believes will somehow preserve and help it heal. True forgiveness transcends our human nature and opens us to the divinely inspired state of grace offered to mankind. Forgiveness is the only thing that will compensate for the awesome, sometimes irrevocable consequences of freewill. It is also the key to spiritual, mental, and physical well-being. If you think about it, Christ's whole life and ministry were about forgiveness. His life focused on showing us the tremendous power and critical ramifications contain within forgiveness.

Each day, we are faced with all kinds of transgressions committed by and against one another. With lies, betrayal, and injury only some of the ways we cause each other pain. The list of ways to hurt one another is as long as mankind is old. Consequently, without the gift of forgiveness we end up emotionally crippled, and worse yet, bitterness and resentment end up feeding the spoors of psychological and spiritual cancer.

Forgiveness is essential to true freedom. While one has to live with the consequences of an offense, and the past cannot be changed, we have a choice of the emotions that we dwell within each day. We can choose bitterness and the insidious physical deterioration caused by the unforgiven burden, or we can ask God into our hearts to free us from the suffering that has been inflicted upon us.

It becomes a matter of truly accepting God as real. We must accept Him in such a way as to know that He will deal with each and every one of us in His perfect way. No one can truly forgive until they know God is there and that His justice is sufficient.

How long we allow the past to affect our daily lives is a choice we must each personally make. Many people face each new day with thoughts of animosity and hatred. Consequently, they can't help extending those harmful emotions into their personal relationships. They literally infect their future with the deep unresolved issues of the past. Their lives end up with hurt piled onto hurt, and pain reinforcing pain. Eventually, those sour emotions gather strength until they hatch unconscious self-destructive thoughts and actions. I also believe that the dark spiritual forces move through this bitterness and pain and ultimately try to project it onto others. Unforgiveness is one of the main spiritual portals through which evil enters this realm and affects our lives

Forgiveness is the power to stop extending the pain. Not only does it truly heal, but it literally closes the door from the dark realm to this one. By releasing the burden to God's righteousness the pain is no longer spread to others or those we love.

I've come to the conclusion that within each of our inner-consciousness, our spirit if you will, there is a part of us that thrives on truth, love, and forgiveness. Unfortunately, when the injury to the soul is severe enough, many turn to hatred and animosity in a deluded effort to strengthen and recover their loss. We see this manifested through revenge and retaliation. When feelings of hatred, helplessness, and frustration are held in a person's heart there is room for little else. Within that person a conflict ensues between those negative self-serving emotions of the ego and the unconscious truth that knows it must bring to light the consequences of those destructive feelings. The psychological battle that results from this inner-conflict can become so intense that it manifests in physical ailments such as ulcers, high blood-pressure, tremors, anxiety attacks, or chest pains, just to name a few.

This psychological distress can also trigger other diseases as it lowers the immune system's ability to fight back. Needless-to-say, there are no drugs or medications that will cure the injury to the ego, or the soul, only by accepting God's ability to make all things work to His good purpose can this affliction be cured.

Leave judgment to God. Those are His instructions. Keep in mind, that hatred is the most sever form of judgment there is. Do not forgive for the sake of the transgressor; forgive for your own mental health, and the sake and well-being of those who love you. Forgive and you shall be forgiven.

Sometimes, the most difficult person to forgive will be yourself. I know from experience how true that can be. I felt responsible for the pain and hardship I placed on the people that I loved. My guilt was almost unbearable, and I feared I would carry it for the rest of my life.

In my heartfelt repentance, I knew that God had forgiven me; however, I could not forgive myself. Then, I found this Bible passage, and each time I read these words I felt a little better. They gave me the hope that in the end love would win the day.

And Jesus said to him, "Simon, I have somewhat to say unto thee.... Two men owed money to a certain creditor. One owed five hundred pence, the other fifty. And when they had nothing to pay, he frankly forgave them both. Tell me therefore, which of them will love him the most?"

Simon answered and said, "I suppose he who was forgiven the most."

And Jesus said unto him, "Thou have rightly judged." Luke 7:41-43

Please forgive me, darling. It is the most precious gift that you can give this contrite and humbled man. It is also the greatest gift you can give yourself.

Now, I give to you...

The Gift

Thinking about my childhood, I can remember few things that I enjoyed better than gifts: Christmas presents, birthday presents, unexpected presents, it didn't matter, presents were a wonderful thing. As a child, I can't really remember anything more memorable than the anticipation produce by Christmas and all of the brightly wrapped packages. I was sure it was possible to die of curiosity, as the whole holiday season was almost more than I could bear.

Every day leading up to Christmas, my brothers and I would inventory the presents to see if any new ones had materialized. Based on their size and shape, we stacked them into neat individual piles as childhood fantasies brought the contents of each precious box to life.

Then when Christmas eve finally arrived Mom and Dad tried to alleviate our stress with the logic that the sooner we went to sleep the sooner morning would arrive. While that seemed reasonable in theory, in actuality, we suffered from the universal childhood affliction called anticipation extremis. A condition brought about by pre-present-opening adrenalin, mixed with a dose of Santa Clause induced endorphins.

Then, long before the dawning of the winter sun, my brothers and I arose to tear into our gifts while Mom and Dad sat back delighted just to watch.

Every once-in-a-while, I'd glance over at them to see the smiles on their faces. While this seemed a little strange, as they hadn't opened a single package, I gave it little thought. I had presents to open, with no time for such mysteries.

Sometime during my formative years, I began hearing things like, it's better to give than to receive or the gift is in the giving. While this sounded good, I couldn't help thinking: *are they crazy, giving a gift is better than getting one? I don't think so.* I certainly had news for them. Nothing was better than getting a present. However, if they thought that giving something away, especially to me, was the best thing, I felt we could probably work this out. From my young perspective this looked like the making of a perfect relationship. They could gladly give me presents and I would happily receive them.

Time marched on. With children of my own, I have found there are few things in life that fill me with more satisfaction and contentment than to see them happy. To empathize with their anticipation before Christmas, and to hear their squeals of joy and laughter as they open their gifts gave me a deep sense of fulfillment. Their happiness moved me far more than any feeling of pleasure that I derived from receiving some material gift. Life had come full circle, and now that I am on the giving end, I sometimes feel that I tapped into that magical source of joy and contentment that used to be a mystery. It took awhile, but I finally realized that it was not the gift, but the love behind the giving from which life flowed.

There is another kind of gift, the gift of kindness. While I have received gifts of kindness many times in my life, one stands out above all the rest.

One snowy night, before the advent of cell phones, my car slid off into the ditch of a desolate country road. After quite sometime, a man in a truck stopped and offered greatly needed assistance. He was a Godsend. He pulled my car out of that ditch and got me on my way.

As I thanked him profusely, I reached for my wallet to pay him for his effort. He held up his hand, smiling as he said, "No, I don't want your money."

Insisting, I said, "Please take it! I don't know what I would have done if you hadn't come along."

Once again, he said, "No." Telling me of a time when he was in a similarly bad situation, and a stranger helped him. When he also tried to repay the stranger for his help, the stranger told him to keep his money but accept this debt: "You must help ten others for the help I have given you." Then as the man who helped me turned to go back to his truck, he said, "You are one of my ten, and if you really want to repay me, you will now help ten others."

I gratefully promised him that I would.

What I didn't expect was that each time I repay my debt, and pass it on to whomever I've helped, I receive in return an emotional jewel; one that not only radiates in gratitude, but also sparkles in the eyes of those who accept their debt, as they comprehend the wonderful ramifications.

We have so many gifts to give each other: the gift of time, the gift of sharing, or the gift of listening that shows someone how much you really care. I'm convinced that giving of yourself and serving others transcends the human experience and creates an entry into the spiritual realm. When we open each of our hearts and offer up the unconditional gift of love, I am convinced that in that instant of emotional outpouring we are closer to God than at any other time. It is in those moments of angelic revelation that my heart tells me of the most precious gift of all: the gift of life. And that is something that should never, ever be denied.

How Far the Journey

So much of life seems to be a game of opposites. I've learned that what makes me whole or gives me a sense of completeness is the understanding of how those opposites strive to bring about my spiritual destiny, a destiny that will eventually unify each of us in our shared spiritual heritage.

Every state of being has its counterpart. Black has its white, hot its cold, and dark its light. The yin has its yang, and what would a man be without a woman. For us to truly understand the goodness of God, the evil of satan is somehow necessary.

Psychology highlights the separation between the conscious and unconscious mind. The Bible offers us the distinction between spirit and soul. In either case one is tuned to this natural world, and the other dwells in a world beyond conscious understanding. To concentrate solely on the conscious mind or soulish realm while ignoring the subconscious or spiritual realm creates a void in which God is absent. The consequence of this life style is that we fail to grasp or move toward our divine destiny.

In my past I allowed myself to get so caught up in the material world that I focused on acquiring wealth and collecting people. I completely ignored my spiritual needs. I suppressed my unconscious warning signals, and I blocked any guidance from my spiritual side connecting me to God.

The odd part was that at the same time I ignored what was important, I yearned for exactly that which I was missing.

As far back as I can remember, even childhood, I have been looking for something.

That elusive "something" kept itself shrouded in obscurity. When it did make an appearance it came in the form of a yearning anxiety--a restlessness cloaked in curiosity. It seemed that the answers to the meaning of life had to be out there—somewhere. I felt that if I looked hard enough, long enough, and in enough places throughout the world, I would uncover some special secret, a key or a Rosetta stone that would unlock the portals to life's meaning.

The fact that I didn't have the slightest clue to what I looked for was no deterrent. Blind and directionless, I sailed wherever the emotional winds blew. The cost was of little consequence to one on so noble a quest--a journey meant to enlighten my inner consciousness and provide me the true meaning of life.

Time as they say marched on with many lessons learned. Lesson like having enough consideration for those around me to warn them of this personality trait that fueled my unrest, and that I felt driven to search for I knew not what.

My unfulfilled yearning continued to grow. I sought out professions in which travel was required. I regularly visited exotic lands, met new people, and learned strange customs. Sometimes I even felt that the answers were close at hand. I could almost sense them within my mental grasp. Only to have those feelings evaporate like the mist as the morning sun rose.

Mile after hundreds of thousands of miles I traveled taking in one wondrous site after another, and feeding my consciousness with all sorts of strangeness and curiosities. I participated in a cornucopia of mind and body altering activities. Somewhere between shots of tequila and peyote buttons, I concluded that the more experiences I acquired the higher the percentage for discovering life's meaning. But that attitude only offered a ride on the Merry-go-round of unfulfillment. Time after time, the brass ring of enlightenment always remained just out of reach.

Eventually, my unending quest grew wearisome. Without even realizing it mental and physical fatigue settled in. No matter how hard I tried my efforts produce no fruit to nourish my inner being. Even with my life filled with all the trapping of material success, I found little inner peace and even fewer answers. The question of life's meaning remained unanswered, yet burned to be resolved.

F. Edward Marx   To Mandi, with Love

I grew tired. The quest had cost me my passion for life. I had seen, done, and forgotten more adventures than most people ever dream of, yet I still felt no closer to my goal.

My disillusionment gained a life all it's own and eventually turned into professional issues, alcohol abuse, financial and marital problems. It was all I could do to muddle through each day as I spiraled above the drain into the abyss of apathy.

I questioned God.

I questioned His plan, and if life had any real meaning at all.

Then in a moment of profound sincerity, I opened my heart and released this prayer: Dear God, is this all there is to life? I feel like I could be a tool. You must know how to use me. Can You use me, Lord, or is this all there is?

At the same time I desired to be closer to Him, I took the final steps away from him. In a cloud of alcohol abuse and what I have come to learn as clinical detachment, I brought His wrath into my life.

His discipline was swift, complete, and irreversible. Overnight, I lost my family, my home on the water, my job, my honor and self-respect. The boredom that had been my nexus was replaced with mind-bending emotional pain, bottomless sorrow, and grief. Fueled by despair, I faced a completely uncertain future. God's hammer blow had struck ending the life I'd lost interest in. The life I'd taken so for granted.

Left with literally nothing, my selfish ego, based on pride, arrogance, and manipulation had been shattered. Who I was crashed against life's granite bottom. The life I'd built was gone and cast irretrievably into oblivion. All that was left was my desperate humanity and the spiritual part of me that I had never before been able to recognize. Reduced to ego-less being, my personality could no longer skew my perception of reality. Somehow, God had bared my soul and laid it open to searing self-examination. He forced me into a connection of an inner awareness without the interferences from my pride filled self.

The magnitude of my loss on top of the realization of the pain that I placed on those I loved left me devastated. My anguish over hurting the people that I cared for provided the emotional vehicle that transcended this physical world. Incomprehensibly, I was able to go places in my psyche where I'd never before been able to travel. I began to realize there was more to consciousness than what could be seen. My pain offered a never before achieved state of mind separate from the reality that I thought I knew. I'd found an awareness that had been hidden from me under the mask of who I wanted the world to think I was. Once I stopped living the façade that my ego believed and presented to the world, the barrier that kept me from delving into the portion of my humanity that connected me with God was removed. In other words, for the first time in my life, I could truly sense, feel, and hear my spiritual essence. Then, as I gave up my illusion of control, I picked up the Bible and the answers that I had searched for all my life flooded out of those printed pages and into me.

I literally felt, not just comprehended, what Christ was trying to teach us. I began to understand how His example would lead us to God. How Truth, Love, and Forgiveness are the spiritual keys that open our hearts to the kingdom of heaven He spoke of.

My dreams began to offer answers and insights; at time even speeding my spiritual growth forward. What I desperately searched the world for and couldn't find was suddenly given to me when God sat me still. He forced me to turn my attention inward. Finally, my quest had been brought to fruition. For the first time in my life, my yearning thirst was finally being quenched.

What answers did I find?

Like most answers, when found, they seem so simple.

The first and most important is that God truly exists. Fear His wrath and relish His grace. Take it from one who knows, it is a fearful thing to fall into the hands of the living God.

Repentance is the key—the Rosetta stone to spiritual awakening. And true repentance can only be achieved, in a pride-less state of being. Ask God to show you how He sees you and you will realize that you have little or nothing to be proud of on your own.

Humility is the trait that God most cherishes in each of us. Let go of excuses and justifications, as they are the bricks and mortar the ego uses to build its fortress of illusions.

Christ showed us the way. Each step that we take in His footsteps will lead us out of the caves of darkness and up the mountain to enlightenment. He will heal you, comfort you, and give you peace.

Nurture and care for those you love--nothing on this earth is more important.

Allow yourself to become spirit-led—cast ego based perceptions aside.

Open up to Christ's teaching. Spend time with Him daily, not just in your time of need.

Eliminate pride, arrogance, manipulation, and control in your life.

Cultivate Truth, Love, and Forgiveness. Carrying bitterness, fear, or deceit will immobilize you. Instead of moving forward in life and closer to God, you will be chained to the past that you so desperately want to forget.

Service to other is the food of the soul. God's word is the food for your spirit. Feed them both daily.

Selfishness and self-indulgence have exactly the opposite effect you would think. Instead of feeling more fulfilled by all that you accumulate or gather, you will feel emptier. Each of us has a place within that only God can fill, and nothing on this earth will satisfy the space where He belongs.

How far the journey?

Your choices will determine the direction you take. It could be like mine—long and painful; or it could be a simple turn inward, humbly repenting, and surrendering to your spiritual being that will lead you directly to Him. The awareness that following Christ will give you will connect you to your own spirituality, completing your quest. Then your own answers will be forthcoming, and you will begin to understand the potential that God has offered mankind.

The Last Train

It's a wet blustery afternoon. As I look out my window a cold drizzle has made its presence known, yet when I look within all I find is warmth and comfort. Since I've been musing about my Grandfather for the last several days, I would like to tell you a story about him.
So, as I sit here sipping a hot cup of coffee and savoring my memories, I offer you this fond rememberence.

Most of my childhood was a time of wonder and a time of peace, but being somewhere between the age of six and self-awareness, I held little esteem for such things.

The rail-bed gravel crunched and rattled under our feet as Grampa and I walked toward our familiar outpost. Feeling the sun's warmth on my face, I shaded my eyes and gazed up toward the blazing orb.

"Grampa, why is the sun so hot?"

"Well, the sun is a huge ball of flaming gas and that fire is what gives us the light and heat that makes it possible for us to live on this earth."

"Why is the sky blue?"

"That's because as the sunlight passes through our atmosphere much of it gets absorbed by the gases and dust in the air. Then, since the color blue is the longest visible wavelength that we can see, less of it is filtered out, and that is why the sky looks so blue."

"Why is the grass green?"

"That has to do with chlorophyll and photosynthesis. Plants and grass eat sunlight. Photosynthesis is how grass eats sunlight, and the green chlorophyll is the light turned into food."

"Eat sunlight?"

"Yep, light is food for plants."

"Oh."

Arriving at the weather-beaten board that spanned two old milk crates, we sat and waited for the train that would soon pass.

"Grandpa, can a train go a hundred miles and hour?"

"Some can, but not a freight train."

"How come?"

"Because they carry lots of heavy stuff."

"What kind of stuff?"

Grandpa pointed down the track.

A single round light hung magically in the air. A shadowy shape began to form as the familiar distant rumble rolled into my ears.

"Do you think it's a long one, Grandpa?"

"It could be fifty cars or more."

"I think it's forty."

Ambitiously flashing its lights to alert the empty intersection, the railroad-crossing signal clanged to life.

The ground began to shudder.

The onrushing giant sounded its warning blast. The volume carried by the pressure wave sliced through me.

Rustling leaves swirled about as the passing wind bristled through my hair.

The behemoth thundered by, its pounding vibrato a symphony of power.

Grandpa lifted his hand and waved.

The engineer spied our greeting. As he again triggered that mighty horn, I cringed from the volume of his deafening "Hello."

Counting the pulsing rhythm of each passing car, we settled into the task at hand. One, two, three…forty-five, forty-six, another wave to the man in the caboose, and our task was complete.

""Forty-seven, you were closet, Grandpa."

"We were both pretty close."

"What's the longest train ever?"

"I'm not sure. But I've seen some trains with more than a hundred cars."

"Wow! Can we wait for another one?"

F. Edward Marx   To Mandi, with Love

"Sure."

Grandpa never tired of waiting for trains with me. He never tired of my endless questions. All I ever noticed was his patience and the light I lit in his eyes.

Later that summer, my territorial range increased and I found some playmates down the street. Their impish appeal overshadow thundering locomotives and the intervals of endearment that Grandpa and I shared—there would always be another train.

The years passed, and as my life became my own, I saw Grandpa less and less. Then he was gone.

Now I look back on those faceless playmates and remember nothing more of them then their existence. But, the flush in his cheeks, the sparkle in his eyes, and his gentle countenance are still with me.

I miss you, dear man. How I wish we could share on more train.

Vi-Lent

Mandi, someday you will have children of your own. Chances are that you will also have the misfortune of having boys. Just maybe, when you are at your wits end because of something they say or do you'll remember this little story about my Mom.

Before I give the wrong impression, my mother, Violet (her friends call her Vi) is one of the sweetest, kindest ladies that have graced this earth. In fact, after raising my two brothers and me, she should be anointed to Sainthood. Today, when the grandchildren visit Grandma Vi, she instantly transforms them into little Princes and Princesses, catering to their every whim. She makes them special dinners, takes them shopping or to the zoo, and of course scattered through out the house, there is candy in every bowl. As far as I can tell, the only mistakes my mother ever made was to give birth to three hulking sons. With my youngest brother and his friends responsible for conjuring the nickname of Vi-lent.

It's hard to imagine, but I may have had something to do with helping Mom acquire this moniker. Even as a teenager, I towered over her diminutive stature. She'd ask me to take out the garbage and I'd say, "Sure Mom, right after the next commercial." Then, after three days of countless request to complete that simple chore, her tolerance would wane, naturally upsetting her ever so slightly. Finally, she'd come to the realization that no words existing in the English language had the power to break my spell of slothfulness, and knowing that she'd only hurt her hand if she tried to smack me into activity, she came up with this neat little motivational device—otherwise known as the broom handle.

After hearing my hundredth or so excuse, she could take it no longer. Instinct drove her to grab the motivator and hurtle herself into the living room flailing the broom handle at me with enough intensity and vigor to impress a Samurai warrior. This always got my attention.

F. Edward Marx   To Mandi, with Love

After a couple of laps around the inside of the house with the motivator doing its job, Vi-lent slowed down enough to allow me to stop and grab the garbage on my way out the door. Now that I think about it, anyone witnessing this ritual and not being privy to my three days of ignoring my mother's request might just get the wrong impression.

Mom wasn't always called Vi-lent. There was a time when she was a calm, lovely young woman of charm, wit, and grace. Unfortunately, I never really knew that lady. For some inexplicable reason she began to change shortly after I was born. Psychology suggest that when accumulated over time, a number of small, seemingly insignificant things can eventually have an impact on someone's personality, but that's just a theory. I find it a little hard to believe that my two Tasmanian devil cloned brothers and I could have had that much affect on her.

Of course, there was that time that she waited until I had grown past the grabbing every thing off the shelf stage to return her cherished Hummel figurine collection to its display case. Within a few hours, I managed to throw a wild pitch fastball right through the cabinet, wiping out the entire collection more efficiently than an earthquake measuring 7.5 on the Richter scale. Now that I'm thinking about it, I wonder if the time I accidentally shot our new TV with my BB gun might have had any effect on her? No, probably not.

As the years went by, my mother seemed to develop certain nervous tendencies. You would think that sitting in a quiet house sewing and looking out the window while watching her boys play driveway hockey would have a soothing effect on a person. You wouldn't think that one little croquette mallet that slipped out of my hand and sailed across the yard in a perfect arc would have bothered her that much. Just because it crashed through the window and covered her in shattered glass shouldn't have had a lasting effect on her. I guess it's just one more of those little things that can eventually add up.

All kidding aside, my brothers and I should never have come up with the nickname of Vi-lent, but boys will be boys. And even

- 61 -

though its use was one of affection, you can bet that when we were sick, or hurt, or needed comfort in the middle of the night, we called her by her real name—Mom.

I am truly blessed to have been brought into this world by a woman who only knows how to give a mother's love.

I know your heart Mandi, and you too will be a blessing.

Trip to Alaska

Charlie and I stepped off the plane to meet our buddy Jeff who had moved to Alaska the year before. The three of us were about to embark on a fisherman's dream. Jeff promised us an adventure filled fishing trip on Kodiak Island where we would be catching salmon and crab to our heart's content. With that in mind, we boarded another jet to Kodiak so that we could charter a floatplane and hop over to the remote ocean inlet referred to by the locals as Lack-of-Nookie Bay.

With visions of giant salmon dancing on their tails across the pristine stage of crystalline following rivers, we began loading the floatplane. Since out total weight limit of seven-hundred-and-fifty-pounds include the three of us, we didn't take many supplies: just the essential artery clogging camping staples of bacon, eggs, bread, and our primary sustenance, three cases of beer.

Loaded to the gills, we finished packing the plane. Like true expeditionist, we boldly took off with an unfiled flight-plan that flew us over some of the most rugged mountains on Kodiak Island.

Since I'd become accustomed to flying at the miniaturizing height of thirty-five-thousand-feet, I felt comforted to look out the window and see that in case of an emergency I could just stick out my feet and run along the side of the plane. I leaned toward the pilot so he could hear me over the drone of the straining engine and yelled, "Aren't those mountains a little close?"

He calmly looked over at me hollering back, "Yep, I'm looking for mountain goats. Got me a permit this year, and I'll be damned if I'm gonna climb one of them hills what ain't got no Billy's on it."

Having climbed empty mountains in search of game myself, I couldn't really fault his logic, so I settled back and tried not to think about the crumpled plane lying in a canyon that he'd just pointed out minutes earlier.

We arrive at our destination and landed uneventfully in the small inland harbor connecting us to the Arctic Ocean. After helping off-load our gear and supplies the floatplane pilot waved goodbye and said, "I'll see you in a week."

Standing on the shore of one of the most remote place on the globe, watching our only link to civilization disappear, I realized that until he returned we were completely isolated and out of contact with the rest of the world. This meant that if we didn't want to starve, one of the first things we needed to do was catch a crab dinner. We mounted the outboard motor that Jeff materialized out of the weeds, and on about the hundred-and-fiftieth pull, it coughed to life.

We eagerly loaded up the sixteen-foot aluminum boat for the trip into Lac-of-Nookie Bay ready to retrieve a crab-pot for our fresh seafood dinner. Just as we're about to launch, Jeff ran up on shore and grabbed an old coffee can.

"What is that for?" I asked.

Jeff smiled and with only a hint of antagonism said, "The boat has a couple of small holes in it and someone has to bail."

Not that I am a stickler for such details, but as we motored out to the middle of the bay, with the wind blowing out toward the Arctic Ocean, in a boat with holes in it, I noticed the lack of any oars or paddles.

"Where are the oars in case the motor quits?" I asked.

With the gleam in his eyes of a true adventurer, or a fool, he replied, "There aren't any."

We continued out to sea, toward the horizon, until we finally arrived at a small rubber float that marked a five-foot diameter steel crab trap that laid fathoms below on the ocean floor.

Jeff yelled above the motor and the wind, "Grab the rope and start pulling."

As I tried to pull the rope, my hands slipped along the ice-cold slime encrusted coating covering the rope.

Charlie grabbed a hold, and together, standing side by side in the small fishing boat, we tempted the fates to cast us overboard into the frigid Artic water.

We heaved and ho'd on that slimy strand for at least twenty minutes until our fingers became frozen, red, curled, barely able to close pieces of flesh. With about a 100 feet of coiled rope all over the bottom of the boat Jeff yelled above the wind, "Don't let go, you have the rope wrapped around your leg and the weight of the crab pot will yank you over." After a solid half hour of hand numbing, back breaking effort we finally got the crab pot up and into the boat. Low and behold, it had one small crab in it. Now added to my list of ways to die out there, like exposure when the motor quits and we're blown out to sea or falling overboard and freezing to death in Arctic waters, was starvation. Charlie and I looked at each other in horror as Jeff said, "Well, I guess we better just pull up another one." With vision of pulling up half the crab pots in the bay, Charlie and I began hauling in what seemed like piece of the Titanic. I looked back at Captain Bly who steered the boat with one hand while bailing with the other and notice a slight smirk that conveyed the thought, having fun yet boys.

While we broke our backs trying to raise this next steel crab pot, Jeff tried to make us feel better by assuring us that it was full of crabs. Then under his breath he chuckled, "Or, it's just a bigger steel pot." Fortunately just as Captain Bly's crew was about to mutiny, the crab pot broke the surface and was full of the biggest, liveliest Dungeness crabs I had ever seen.

Jeff had told us all about the little rustic cabin that we would be staying in. It was all that he promised, remote, rugged, a magnificent view of the mountains all around us and right on the water. The sea froth actually hit the cabin when the wind really cranked up, which happened all the time. That hovel was all he said it would be, and more. Like when the wind blew the cabin lifted off it's stilts and rocked backward, then when the wind stopped blowing the cabin fell back down with a thump. While this was mildly disturbing during mealtime, going to bed was a whole other problem. I felt like I was trying to fall asleep on the edge of a cliff. Just as I dosed off, the cabin would rock back, hesitate for a moment then thump down. The effect on my half-asleep brain felt like I rolled over an edge and dropped off.

He also forgot to tell us about things like the smells. Whoever used the cabin last had left some eggs out and forgot about them. So after a couple of hours of searching the cabin high and low, we finally found the origin of that terrible smell and threw them out. We were so relived to be rid of those nasty little things that we didn't give much thought to where we threw them, which was downwind into the bushes. What we rationalized later was that those odoriferous rotten eggs were to bears what advertising for a free seafood buffet is for people. We didn't know it at the time but we were calling, more like summoning, the bears from as far as the wind carried the smell of those small but obnoxious, broken eggs.

After my evening medicinal six-pack that helped me go to sleep while repeatedly falling off the side of a cliff, I awoke in the middle of the night to take a leak. Grabbing one of the chemical light sticks that we had in ample supply, I thought, *what a wonderful little invention, just by bending and shaking it I have all the light I need.* As the chemical light stick cast it eerie glow that radiated around me in a globe of deep blue light, I ventured outside. Taking a few steps away from the cabin, I almost tripped on a Kodiak grizzly (the largest known carnivore living today, I might add).

I screamed.

The bear peed. And even though Kodiak grizzlies consider themselves to be on the top of the food chain, I think that the blood curdling vocals emanating out of my glowing blue luminescence was more than the bear was prepared for with each of us disappearing in opposite directions.

I wasn't sure how frightened the bear might have been, but once I could actually distinguish one heartbeat from the next I noticed that I didn't have to go to the bathroom anymore.

As I lay in my bunk rocking and thumping with the cabin, I thought about the events of the first day. *This was going to be a long week.*

The Night of the Dummy

You and Bobby were fast asleep when a couple of your mother's friends stopped by. Little did I know that their simple visit would unleash a havoc that changed all of our lives. That mayhem had a name of course, and it answered to Max. This was the night we got Maxwell. Also know as Max the Dummy.

Your mother had been talking about this dog for months. Every time she went to Cara's house she'd return earnestly explaining how Max put his head in her lap and gave her that brown-eyed, black lab look that pleaded, "Please take me home with you."

Of course, what your mother didn't realize was that black labs only have two looks. The first and most often used is can I have some of what you are eating, and the other lesser known look is please take me home with you. Since your mother wasn't eating anything, she naturally got the other look.

Crystal had been softening me up about this dog long before Cara came to visit that fateful night. It didn't take long before the conversation turned to how Max was doing. Cara explained that she had too many dogs and really needed to get rid of one. This prompted your mother to resume coercing me by saying things like: "I promise, you won't have to do anything. I'll feed him and clean up after him every single day."

I himmed and hawed, considering that once reality set in, I would end up with the care and feeding, not to mention the vet bills for this animal. Then as if on cue Cara said," If I don't find Max a home, he'll have to go to the pound."

One look from your mother let me know that it was all over but the poop scooping. So on a cold February night, at about one in the morning, we gathered coats and gloves and ventured into the night.

Standing in Cara's kitchen, I watched as she opened the door and in tumbled three mud-encrusted balls of fur. Immediately, your mother began her urgent plea, "Can we keep him, pleasssssse?"

Knowing that if I said no, I would end up on the list of scoundrels somewhere between Ebenezer Scrooge and the Marquis de Sade, I broke down and relented with a half-hearted, "Okay."

With a borrowed leash around Max's neck, we headed out the door thinking how pleased Max would be in his new home. It was obvious how much he liked us because every time I stopped petting him, he'd put his muddy head under my hand so that I'd be forced to pet him some more. However, the second we began to leave with Max in tow, he decided that he wanted no part of these strangers. As soon as I began leading Max off into the unknown, he slammed on his brakes. At seven months old, he had no intention of leaving home and mother.

Even for Black Labs, Max was big for his age. Realizing he wasn't going to get into the car on his own, I reluctantly decided to pick him up. Instantly, he became a flailing, squirming, seventy-pound bundle of mud and fur. At least I hoped it was mud. Since I had little experience in putting black labs through back doors, I had no idea that such a creature could render itself into so many shapes and postures. As I strained to get him close to the opening of the car door, Max effectively contorted into a spread-eagle, stiff as a board, four-pointed star that in no way resembled any known shape for a dog, and certainly nothing that fit into an opening of a car. Feeling like something was about to 'pop' in the middle of my spine, I struggled to maintain my hold on the squirming mass of flesh. Your mother tried to help by bending his legs back into their original position, but it immediately became apparent that Max's four legs outnumbered your mother's two hands.

After a five minute, back breaking, struggle trying to fit a wild-eyed, star peg into a round hole, I closed the door on the newest, all be it, reluctant member of the family.

The whole way home, I figured he'd be happy and relieved to get out, but that was not to be. As soon as we arrived, Max immediately seized up into his stiff legged four-pronged position that once again created an opportunity for me to experience what a hernia felt like.

I suppose it was possible that in Max's mind he had been captured by evil dognappers bent on torment and torture. Then, as I carried him up the stairs, still the stiff legged dog-star, his worst fears were confirmed. We gave him a bath.

After his cleansing, Max roamed around the house sniffing everything. I couldn't help get the impression that he figured there was no end to the mischief he could get into and that this place might just work out.

The next morning when he met you and Bobby, I think he knew that everything was going to be just fine.

The Freedom of Truth

I'm not sure why but it seems that lies are a part of human nature. We all tell lies, no matter how hard we may try not too. It seems that a little white lie now and then is inevitable. Yet, I'm absolutely convinced that I must strive to live in the truth. This can be difficult and challenging, but I've learned that the truth is where true freedom dwells.

It is so easy to accept the skewed perceptions of the ego. These illusions are the lies by which each of us distorts or tries to change the perception of reality—either our own or someone else's. While it may not seem to be the case, these lies are incredibly stifling and burdensome. With each one adding to the psychological cancer that infects and digest health and wholesomeness.

I can offer a glimpse of this idea in the example of the dieter's delusion. I have actually convinced myself that by going on a diet tomorrow I can eat whatever I want today. In reality, all I accomplished was to add to my prison of fat, while my ego maintained that escape was only a day away. Then each additional day that I failed to see my own delusion, I added more tissue to the walls that restricted me.

One of the wonders of the truth is that it can be searched out and embraced at any time. While simple, this concept is not necessarily easy. In fact, seeing through the distortions of the ego could be one of the most difficult aspects of a person's life. For most of us our ego is so strong and deeply imbedded that it will fight the truth to the very end, and we don't even realize it is doing this. Ultimately, we end up in a prison of our own making, and the really crazy part is we can't even see the bars This, of course, is the essence of denial, and the real danger of denial is that it often precedes self-destruction.

One of the reasons why I believe that God places such high regard on humility is because there is a self-less sense to it. The reality being that I am much less than my ego would have me believe. I have learned the value of humility from which a deeply profound sense of strength flows. Show me a truly humble man or woman, and I will show you a person who lives in the truth, free of denial, delusions, and deceit. A person secure in self and God. However, show me a pride-filled human being, and I will show you someone for whom the truth is only a shadow. A person full of the self-hyphenations like self-sufficient, self-aware, and self-centered. The sad part is that self-filled person's version of reality is all that matters. He or she dosen't realize and often doesn't care that their connection to the Spirit of God is suppressed or blocked. Unfortunately, this state of being is where evil has all the room it needs to maneuver.

Our counterpunch to the dark one is to strive to always find and tell the truth. Then the truth begins to open our lives to the realm where love and forgiveness dwell.

Living in the truth will literally change a person's personality. Since we lie to cover actions and thoughts that are wrong or we feel ashamed of. The need for a lie is usually found in not wanting to be caught or to deter consequences. In other words, a lie results from doing something that should not have been done in the first place. Living in the truth requires the need to change behaviors that caused the need for lies or secrecy. This fundamental change is where the magic begins.

Mandi, if you ever wish to soar with the eagles of the mystic world you will need the wings of a clear conscience, unfettered by the shackles and chains of lies and secrets. It is there that the deepest truths of consciousness can begin to lift you beyond this physical realm to universes not yet understood, but no less real.

Always remember that the best relationships exist on a foundation of trust. In the light of the truth people can go about their daily lives not worrying about the skeleton in the closet, or trying to remember what was told to whom. True freedom can never be achieved as long as one lives with the haunting fear of the truth unexpectedly emerging. The consequence of revealed shame will feel like a sharpened sword dangling by a single thread over the top of your head. And you'll never be sure when that thread might snap. Then when that thread of secrecy does break it's odd how the ego handles that sinking feeling of having been caught in a lie. Its first response will be to justify and cover itself by adding more lies to the original. Sadly, each additional fabrication will infect more of a person's goodness and light until there is little if any left. The stress, anxiety, and deterioration of one's general health seem like a high enough price to pay; however, the costs are even higher. The loss of self-esteem, and credibility are commodities that once lost are very, very difficult to regain.   The importance of your integrity can never be understated, and when someone fells lied to, they may never really trust you again.

When you reject the desires of the ego and deal only in the truth no matter how uncomfortable it may be, the truth will weather the storm and stand the test of time. I'm reminded of one of Christ's most profound teachings: "And the truth will set you free." Free from the shackles of guilt. Free from the ego's prison of trying to remember all the lies, and free to let your spirit soar on its journey toward higher consciousness. The deeper you venture into the truth the stronger you'll find your link that connects you to God.

Seek your own truth, Mandi, and remember that the wings of truth are designed as one size fits all. I have found that those wings lift me above those who would try to cause me harm, and they also set me free from the biggest problem of all…myself.

F. Edward Marx   To Mandi, with Love

A Trip to the Mall

In one of my weaker moments, I suggested to all you kids: "Why don't we go to the mall and have Coney Island hot dogs and see a movie.

"Yeah!!!   Great!   Let's go," each of you enthusiastically responded.

"What about homework?" I inquired.

"Oh, it's all done," came the unanimous reply.

Kids are like that, suggest something even remotely like fun and rest assured homework will be instantly completed well into the next century.   On the other hand, when I suggested something like, why don't we go outside and cut the lawn, trim, rake and pull weeds, I got the distinct impression that each of you were working on your doctoral thesis. Something about the new element you discovered that was soon to be added to the Periodic Table.

If I close my eyes I can almost picture a family out for the evening with all of us sitting together chatting while waiting for our order of Coney dogs and chili fries to arrive. Something a modern Norman Rockwell might portray with bright-eyed children happily sitting with hands properly placed on the table and only the slightest hint of mischief in their eyes. Of course that's not exactly accurate, and for those unfortunate enough to be seated in the booth next to us, they witnessed an unchoreographed, but well rehearsed, seating contest that started with who is sitting next to whom, followed by jousting and crawling under the table for the seat next to the window. The eventual conclusion ended with the smallest child in tears because she wanted to sit next to me.   All I could do was smile at the people around us, and to anyone else who might be listening say, "They're not all mine."

As the waitress approached, eyeing out booth that is littered with torn napkins and a spilled glass of water, I recognized the look of:

Mister, you better leave a tip that covers not only cleaning but remodeling as well.

When the soft drinks arrived, you guys, who can't ever do anything together, simultaneously, as if on cue, grab your straws, pop them on the table and blow the wrappers off. This created a short but very noticeable display of wrapper-rockets streaming toward the ceiling over our booth.

The rest of dinner was pretty typical: a Coney dog with everything ended up in a lap, one more drink spilled, and the finale, a $35.00 bill for hot dogs (tip not included).

Since we had about thirty minutes to kill before going into the movie, I thought I could relax next to a large sculptured fountain while letting you guys ride the escalator.

No problem, right.

Wrong, I barely sat down when I looked over to see Chelsea, who was about six at the time, climbing the rock sculpture. Somehow she'd managed to get upside down, facing the ceiling stretched out like an inverted crab. She was moving along with one hand and foot on the sculpture, and the other hand and foot on the pool's retaining wall with the fountain flowing beneath her back. Before I could get up to either save her or sell her to the lowest bidder, her foot slipped off the rock and in she goes up to her knees. As I arrived at the wishing pool, she calmly steps out of the water and says, "Boy those rocks sure are slippery."

As I sat down to begin drying her off, I heard this commotion at the top of the escalator. Mandi, I don't know how you did it, but somehow you'd gotten yourself wedged between the moving handrail and the guard-post that was placed there to keep anyone from getting wedge between the escalator and the wall. The handrail looked to be trying to eat you by rubbing off one layer of skin at a time. After I turned up my pacemaker and pulled you from the child-eating escalator, you were a little shaken up, but other wise no worse for the wear. I on the other hand was considering the need for an EKG.

I wrung out Chelsea's pant legs, and noticed on the clock that the movie was about to begin.

Time sure flew when we were having fun.

The Glamour of Travel

Having traveled most of my adult life, first in the military then as a business professional, I often heard people say things like: "It must be nice to travel so much," or "I wish I could go to Spain." Well, it's been my experience that there are almost as many mishaps as miles between exotic locations. And you know that mint that finds it's way onto the hotel pillow each night. Well, it's highly over rated.

If you'd like a for-instance, I originally wrote this while on a twenty-hour, over-booked, full-coach plane ride to Asia. Fortunately, the crying child was at least twelve rows behind me, and I could almost ignore it.

People seem to think that every hotel I stay in has a pool, where each evening I can be found leisurely kicked back drinking a MaiTai. Little do they know of the hazards that the third hotel in as many nights can present. While waking in the middle of the night to get a drink of water may not seem dangerous, I'm convinced that after I go to sleep the furniture rearranges itself. This, of course, causes me to trip in the dark, stub my toe, and ricochet into the protruding edge of the wall.

One of my favorite travel challenges is the not-often-thought-of adversity of remembering my fourth rental car of the week. The trial begins when I walk out to the parking lot and look out over a sea of automobiles, only to realize that I have no idea what kind of car I last drove. Fortunately, the thoughtful rental car people have placed license plate numbers on the key chain, and it becomes a simple matter of time as I walk up and down the rows of parked cars. Someday, some inconsiderate thief is going to steal my rental car, leaving me aimlessly wandering in a parking lot, muttering to myself, "It must be here somewhere."

F. Edward Marx   To Mandi, with Love

Travel light, that's my motto. At least it was until I split the seam of my only pants on an overnight trip. I am now burdened with a tiny sewing kit.

Never and I repeat never leave your hotel room without a key. Of course, most people can just go down to the front desk and ask for another. However, there are exceptions, like the morning I stuck my head out of the door to see if the hotel had delivered a morning paper. Then after picking it up, I noticed that right across the hall brewed a fresh pot of coffee. Since I hadn't had my shower or my first sip of morning brew, I thought how nice it would be to just sneak over and grab a quick cup. For those who haven't had this experience it's hard to imagine the gut-wrenching sound a hotel door makes as it closes behind you. Especially when you are standing in the hallway with nothing more on (or should that be moron) than a towel.

When people ask me what is the most exciting thing about my travels, I get the feeling that they are expecting an answer like hiking through the rain forest or touring ancient architecture. After careful consideration, I have come to the conclusion that nothing quite compares with the true sense of adventure that comes from using public restrooms.

In many countries separate Men and Women's facilities aren't always available; a simple fact that I became painfully aware of one afternoon in a quaint bistro in Paris. Having noticed a guy exit through swinging doors, I correctly concluded that he'd just left the Men's room.   What I didn't conclude was that ladies used the same facility. So, while I attempted to make room for another beverage these two young Mademoiselles walked in. As they passed between me and the back wall—without so much as an excus`e moi—one of them accidentally bumped into me. Then, they casually strolled over and disappeared into a stall without their conversation so much as skipping a beat. I, on the other hand, slipped into a slight state of shock, which had an adverse effect on the functioning of my plumbing.

How about walking into an open-air restroom that is really no more than a ditch surrounded by five-foot-high walls. Which if you are five foot-tall Filipino, is just fine. However, as a six foot tall American, I found myself standing there with my head sticking out above the top of the wall, trying to look casual. This wouldn't have been so bad if I hadn't been right across the street from an open air market where about fifty little old toothless ladies were sitting, selling their goods and wares. Then just as I began to accomplish the task at hand, as if on cue, they all looked straight at me and smiled. Needless to say, those toothless little old ladies were quite intimidating. To this day, I fail to see the entertainment value that my red face seemed to provide.

A frequent Asian custom is that of head-boys, which in many third world economies is considered a good job. Usually a head-boy is a grown man who takes the cleanliness of his restroom seriously. He also provides clean towels and an assortment of toiletries. On occasion, seeking a good tip, one of them will get a little overly enthusiastic and provide a quick back and neck massage at the exact time I least appreciated his effort. Instead of relaxing me, the massage had just the opposite effect and I could hardly go at all. At first, I thought the fellow didn't realize the anxiety that his massage therapy created, so not wanting him to repeat his service, I tipped him poorly. Upon my return, he once again enthusiastically kneaded my neck and shoulders. It wasn't until the man next to me who gave the head-boy a good tip after not being manhandled that I caught on. Only after my gratuity equaled my anxiety did he leave me alone.

Of course, let's not forget everyone's favorite travel malady-- jet lag. When I arrived in Singapore it was exactly twelve hours difference from my home time zone in Michigan. Not to mention a completely different day. As I sat in a 2:00pm meeting trying to concentrate, my body is at 2:00am rebelling with uncontrollable yawns; along with eyelids that have taken on weight measured in metric tons. A little less than a week later, I get to play biorhythm gymnastics as I return to my home time zone.

Sometimes I can't tell whether it's jet lag or just plain anxiety as I enter a new country. Especially, when the first sign offering directions looks like a three-year-olds finger painting. I suppose I will always find it mildly disturbing to become instantly illiterate.

So the next time you see an advertisement depicting a world traveler sitting in his hotel room Jacuzzi, sipping a glass of wine while working on his laptop, think about all the working stiffs who are fighting jetlag, eating food they can't recognize, and using restrooms with unusual features like footprints painted on each side of a hole. Then, you will begin to appreciate the reality behind the glamour of travel.

F. Edward Marx   To Mandi, with Love

Spring Fishing

We hadn't been fishing for over two months while waiting for the winter's ice to thaw, so when my life long buddy Mac called and told me that his wife Sheri ordered him to get out of the house, I knew it was time to go fishing. Since Sheri is a M. D., she quickly diagnosed that Mac suffered from the common March affliction known as "inhouse-itis." As we called Mitch our other life long buddy and made plans for Saturday, I felt good about participating in a program of therapy, prescribed by a licensed physician. Knowing Sheri, she probably suspected that by getting Mac, Mitch, and I together something would happen and Mac would be cured for at least a month.

March mornings in Michigan can be quite pleasant; however, this wasn't one of them. Clear blue sky can mean one of two things: a sunny pleasant day, or that it's too cold for clouds to form. Typical of our outings, the worst-case scenario was the most common. After loading the boat with all the enthusiasm and anticipation of beginning a new fishing season, we launched toward open water.

"Geez".... Mitch complained, "the boat didn't slide nearly as far as I thought it would."

"I know," I said, "If the ice was just a little thicker the boat wouldn't keep breaking through and we could get out to open water."

Shifting into his analytical mode, Mac, carefully studied the situation. Then in a moment of clarity produced by the mind-numbing cold, he came up with a suggestion. "Just bust holes in the ice for the oars, and we'll be able to plow through like one of the Coast Guard's ice breakers."

Since I rowed, I could tell Mac thought this plan a good one. The only problem was that our fourteen-foot aluminum boat was not exactly designed with ice breaking in mind; therefore you have to be careful about following certain rules. The first rule when breaking ice with a thin metal rowboat is to put as much weight in the back as possible. This will raise the bow so that the boat's weight pushes the jagged ice downward without puncturing a very undesirable hole. The second and most important rule is: make sure it is not your boat. In this case it was my Dad's boat, so we were all in compliance with the second rule.

After about an hour of some seriously strenuous activity that consisted mostly of slapping the oars against ice and water, we broke free.

I looked over at Mac, who with the sweat of exertion or splashed ice water dripping down his face, looked back and said, "Whew, that was a long twenty feet."

Having fished our way back to the far end of the lake, the three of us were standing in the boat delicately casting toward the edge of the ice. Suddenly, one of those strange quirks of nature occurred. To this day I'm not really sure what happened, but the boat rocked to one side. Immediately, Mac and I sat down. Since our quick downward movement was a simultaneous effort our combined weight had the effect of turning the rocking boat into a small catapult. Mitch, whose reaction time lagged behind ours by a fraction of a second, instantly became an involuntary projectile. Now as projectiles go, Mitch didn't travel that far; but the look of astonishment on his mid-flight face confirmed the launch's success. As his expression changed from unbelief to comprehension, Mitch, doing a perfection imitation of the Lipton-ice-tea-plunge-while-holding-a-fishing-pole, disappeared into the chill depths.

Still clutching his rod and reel, he sputtered back to the surface. Which we were wondering about as his bulky winter clothing had been instantly transformed into a weight that could easily anchor the Queen Mary. Until that moment, Mitch had never been known for swiftness or great athleticism, but apparently invigorated, he swam back to the boat in what I am sure would be an Olympic record, if there were such and event as the fully-clothed-three-yard-flail.

Having witnessed Mitch's poor attempt at flight, Mac and I began laughing. Knowing how cold it had to be, we really wanted to help him back into the boat, but it takes all of a person's strength to laugh hysterically. To Mitch's dismay all we could do was hold our sides and let the tears freeze on our faces. Understandable, Mitch failed to grasp the humor of the situation. He very inconsiderately almost tipped us over when he propelled himself up the side of the boat and back in. By not being willing to wait in the frigid water until one of us could help him, he could have capsized the boat and gotten us all wet. Both Mitch and I felt that he displayed a complete lack of regard for the fact that we were still dry. Had either of us been able to speak, we would have given him a good tongue lashing for his lack of consideration.

Eventually, between gasps for air, we suggested that he keep warm by rowing back to shore. Which I thought showed a great deal of sensitivity for our friend. Mac and I certainly didn't want Mitch to freeze solid.

The rest of the day was pretty uneventful. Mitch rowed back at speeds normal clocked by Radar. I locked the keys in the car while it was still running, causing Mac to be re-afflicted with a laughing fit that had him considering medical attention—something about lack of oxygen and heart function. At least, his inhouse-itis had been cured.

All things considered this was a pretty typical escapade for one of our prescribed courses of therapy. I think the lesson here shows just how important it is to find the time to relax and do a little fishing with your friends.

F. Edward Marx   To Mandi, with Love

Humility

Mandi, your battle for life and the operations that you endured have given you a gentleness and humility that has always amazed me. You don't even realize how special you are, which only makes you that much more endearing. God has touched your heart, my darling, never let that go.

Humility was a word barely in my vocabulary. Let alone a trait I possessed or admired. I went so far as to be proud of my arrogance, feeling that I had earned my success and abilities. I now realize that it was that attitude that cost me everything that I ever valued.

I learned the hard way the lesson of pridefulness, but I didn't have to. I could have avoided a lot of pain and anguish if I had only been humble enough to pick up my Bible and read how God feels about pride and arrogance.

When pride cometh then comes disgrace, but with humility comes wisdom. Proverbs 11:2.

Satan's sin was that of pride. He was originally known as Lucifer meaning Giver of Light. Adorned in splendor, He stood before the throne of God as the guardian cherub. Unfortunately, he forgot where that splendor originated in the first place. The Bible tells us in Ezekiel 28:14-17: *You were anointed as a guardian cherub for I so ordained you. You were on the Holy mount of God. You walked among the fiery stones. Your heart became proud on account of your beauty and you corrupted your wisdom because of your splendor. So I threw you to the earth, I made a spectacle of you before kings.*

I didn't know of this Bible passage until after I learned my own lessons. But I guarantee you that pride and arrogance will separate you from God faster than anything else. There is little room for God in a pride-filled heart. And when a person feels superior, it becomes a form of self-worship, eventually leading to the attitude of what need of God have I.

- 84 -

I didn't realize it but I had become my own God. I felt there wasn't anything I couldn't provide for or take care of, nor anything I couldn't do—even breaking God's laws.

I believe that God so cherishes humility that He sent Christ to provide us with the example. He walked this earth in humble servitude to mankind even though His empowerment gave Him every right to rise above those He so faithfully served.

Pride and arrogance are characteristics of the soul. Humility matures in the ego-less realm of the spiritual. Pride is the foundation on which the ego builds, and as long as the ego has its way it will do everything in can to remain in control. The ego will never willing relinquish to matters of the spirit, and I believe this is one of the main reasons why we find it so difficult to connect with God. Recognizing our true place in the universe and what our relationship with God should be would mean giving God control of our lives. And so few are able to surrender. Part of the problem is that most people don't realize that the ego is centered in the soul and focused on an earthly or fleshly agenda; an agenda seldom in line with God's plan for a person's life.

Just as satan allowed pride to corrupt him, I allowed my natural attributes to feed my ego, until I too believed I was something special. Unfortunately, once my ego began to bask in the glow of self-illumination, I lost my empathy, my conscience, and my connection to God. In my arrogance, I forgot where all the things that made me special in the first place came from. I lost track of the fact that I am only a steward of my physical gifts. Attributes of strength, beauty, and intelligence are only temporary, dissipating in power and dimming in brilliance, as we grow older.

As I dwell upon these things this tragedy occurred to me: how much time with God have I lost because I let the gifts He bestowed on me corrupt and block me from touching His inner light?

Humility, on the other hand, opens or enables the precious connection to the divine. It is a timeless, spiritual quality that allows us to remain within God's presence, receiving His grace. I recently read in James that God opposes the proud but gives grace to the humble. That sums up the first part of my life—living in opposition to God. But He has a way of dealing with each of us and He certainly dealt with me. Then, in the sorrow of my shattered life, my humility was born, and a new world opened right before my eyes. It was a world that had always been there but that my ego refused to see. In that moment of forgiveness and grace, I realized that the only thing special about me was that He truly loved me, and that I was infinitely important to Him. In my moment of clarity, I knew that in all of his creation, throughout the universe, there is nothing He cherishes more than each of us. We truly are His children and the love He has for us is beyond our imaginings.

Is there any more sobering a thought than to consider that through freewill He has given each of us control of our soul's eternal destiny?

My humility crystallized when I realized how high the stakes truly are, and how close to the abyss I stood.

Service to others is the food of the soul, but pride and arrogance form a selfish barrier that will keep a person from seeing and understanding the needs of those around him. It was not until humility opened the eyes of my heart that I began to see the light of God's compassion.

As you grow in your abilities, and you begin to understand the effect you have on others, always remember the miracle that you are, and who you truly belong to.

Take my yoke upon you and learn from me for I am gentle and humble in heart, and you will find rest for your souls. For my yoke is easy and my burden light. Matthew 11:29-30.

He could have been crowned an earthly king, however that meant nothing to Him. Alone and humiliated, He paid the ultimate price in order to show us what really matters.

Mandi, you will always be in my prayers. A prayer that asks that neither you nor I ever lose our humility that came at such a dear, dear, price.

F. Edward Marx   To Mandi, with Love

The Test
I said to God, "Look how much I've grown."
Then I waited for His reply.
When a man came up to talk to me,
I spoke of how I was better than he.
But when he was gone, in my heart I knew
I had failed God's test for humility.

F. Edward Marx   To Mandi, with Love

God Meant it for Good

Someday I hope you have the experience of reading something so profoundly moving that you feel it was written with just you in mind. I had such an experience when I read the book titled **God Meant It For Good** by R.T. Kendall. It is a detailed analysis of the story of Joseph as told in the book of Genesis. The concepts that Mr. Kendall puts forth and how they paralleled my own life seem more than just a coincidence.

Joseph was the eleventh son of Jacob, who fathered the twelve tribes of Israel. Jacob honored Joseph as his favorite son by giving him a highly prized coat of many colors. This made Joseph very proud. Joseph also had dreams that his father, mother, and brothers would bow down to him. But instead of keeping those dreams to himself, he flaunted them along with the status his coat held. Joseph also antagonized his brothers by being a tattletale. The Bible says that he regularly brought to his father evil reports of his brothers. So based on his feelings of being something special, Joseph became prideful and arrogant. He set himself apart by feeling superior about his relationship with his father and with God. Among other problems, this attitude caused jealousy within his family.

That idea of setting myself apart and feeling superior resonated deep with my soul. Without a doubt I too am guilty of this behavior.

Then, one day, Joseph's brothers seized an opportunity to get rid of him. They first threw him into a pit and were going to leave him for dead, but eventually they sold him into slavery. And just as effectively as if they had killed Joseph, they ended the life that he once knew.

My selfishness, and arrogance, along with bad decision caused my own life's destruction. And when your mother divorced me and

- 88 -

took twenty-five years of hard honestly earned assets, I felt that my life had ended.

Joseph may not have deserved the severe treatment he received; yet he brought it upon himself. And once I peeled the layers of my life back far enough, I too realized that I had no one to blame but myself.

R.T. Kendall's overall premise is that all that happened to Joseph was part of God's plan not only for Joseph's future, but the future for the whole nation of Israel. He went on to write: *Before we can be of any value, something must happen to us. What is it?*

Whatever it takes to bring us to the place where we see that God gives us a gift for His greater purpose. The very self-esteem to which He appeals needs radical surgery before He in the end can actually use us.

Of Joseph's many gifts were dreams and their interpretation. A gift, I too, feel that I have been given. Someday maybe you will read the novel I wrote that centers on the fulfillment and interpretation of dreams.

When I read chapter four of Mr. Kendall's book, I felt like he had reached into my soul and put my life on paper.

He wrote. *If God puts His finger on you, it is enough to change you, your family, you church—even a nation and the world. The highest compliment a man can ever have is to be tapped on the shoulder by God. When that happens wonderful things are at hand. Yet, when that happens it means that a time of preparation is at hand. This can also be called God's chastising. It is God's way to get the man He has owned ready for His own use. When God puts His finger on you things may get worse before they get better.*

As far as I'm concerned that may be the understatement of the millennia. The darkest and most deeply depressing days of my existence fell upon me overnight. The life I knew was over, and nothing would ever be the same. And while I didn't know it at the time, it would be five long soul searching years before I would emerge whole and newly formed.

Kendall wrote: *The first thing we notice about Joseph's preparations is that it began without notice. A part of what makes chastening chastening is that it comes suddenly and unexpectedly. When our world is shattered and the bottom drops out, it is in fact, the result of the most careful planning by a loving, wise, sovereign God.*

I went from a world-class executive who seemed to have it all, to a homeless, broken man in a matter of twenty-four hours. Never again would I see my beautiful home, or the family that I loved, and just a few short weeks later, my twenty-five year career would come to an end.

The second thing that God puts His finger on is our "sore spot."

In Joseph case his sore spot was symbolized by his coat of many colors, but in the end it was really Joseph's pride that God dealt with.

My pride and arrogance paraded about unbridled, and as I look back on the man I allowed myself to become, all I feel is shame and regret. If I have learned anything in my lessons, it is that God loathes pride and has absolutely no use for it.

I now see the roll that your mother played in my chastising. At first I blamed her, and her greed, and that if she had given family counseling a chance maybe things would have turned out differently. But that would have left my ego intact and in control. Instead when she turned on the faucet of self-pity recruiting all who would listen as to what a monster I turned out to be, she embarked us all on a journey of no return. But, I no longer blame her. I hurt your mother so deeply that in her pain all she could think to do was strike back and exchange hurt for hurt, and grief for grief.

Kendall opened my eyes with these words: *The third thing about Joseph's preparation is this: when God put His finger on him, he underwent the shock of seeing how sinful and frail others were. Joseph knew that his brother's weren't fond of him. But little did he know that they were capable of doing what they did.*

I never dreamed of the lengths your mother would go to accomplish what as she said was, " I am going to get it all."

I now have nothing but remorse for putting those I loved in the position of having to succumb to the flood of primal emotion that washed all truth aside. Never could I imagine that the people I cared so much for and invested my heart and soul into could end up treating me the way things turned out.

Kendall explained: *Before Joseph was ever going to be of use to God, he needed to observe people with a certain objectivity. He could hardly have expected that his own brothers would cast him into a dry pit intending to leave him.*

Kendall continued with: *Why does God want us to see the frailties of other men? The answer lies in Psalm 118:8. "It is better to trust in the Lord than to put confidence in man."*

We must all learn this lesson, but it comes hard.

Mandi, if there is an easier way to learn the lesson of whom to put your confidence in, I heartily recommend trying to find it. Because learning this lesson the hard way is, well, let me put it like this, I'm not sure I could live through another.

The fourth thing God does to a man on whom He puts His finger is to bring Him to a place of apparent despair. They cast Joseph into a pit and left him to die. There was nothing for him to do but pray.

The way God often test our faith is to bring us to places where there is no known precedent. God likes to bring us to impossible situations when, humanly speaking it's the end.

Like Joseph whose brother's sold him into slavery for monetary gain. I too felt abandon and accused due to the motive of greed. Homeless, lost in a torrent of emotion and anxiety, I faced an unknowable and uncertain future. On my knees in a puddle of my own tears, all I knew for certain was that the life I'd been living was over. My world, or the reality that I had created turned to devastation, and all I could see or imagine ahead of me was pain, humiliation, loneliness, grief and tears.

Just as effectively as if I had been cast into a pit like Joseph, I found myself trapped in despair with the darkest days still ahead.

Finally, when God puts His finger on His man, He will bring Him to the point of no return. That is what God did to Joseph. The ten brothers lifted Joseph out of the pit when they saw the Ishmaelites coming. Then they sold him for twenty pieces of silver. There was no turning back for Joseph.

What was accomplished was the impossibility of turning back, and there was absolutely nothing Joseph could do about it. Perhaps the single most important thing that happens to the man God puts His finger on is to bring him to a place where there is no turning back. All he could do was wait and see what God would do next.

The life I knew and everything I cared about vanished. I felt sold out by your mother. Yet, the bottom line was I had no one to blame but myself. Still, there was no going back, no recovery, like Joseph, I was about to step into my spiritual desert and begin an amazing journey that would eventually lead me back into the arms of a loving Father.

The story of Joseph's journey eventually led to his gift of dreams and their interpretation placing him before Pharaoh. Where he went from prison rags to holding the highest office in the land, second only to Pharaoh. There was no way for Joseph to know this, he had to trust God exclusively, but Joseph was about to be tasked with saving the whole civilization of Egypt, along with the emerging nation of Israel, represented by his father Jacob and his eleven other brothers. Through Joseph, God saved the not yet born people of Israel from the impending natural disaster and starvation.

Kendall's book gets its title from what happened twenty-two years after Joseph's ordeal began when he confronted his brothers by revealing that he, the governor of Egypt, is really the brother they sold into slavery all those years earlier. As the brothers bowed to his authority, bringing Joseph's dream to fruition, they trembled over the fate they expected to befall them. Contrary to the ego's needs, Joseph showed just how far God had taken him by offering total forgiveness, compassion, and love for those who deserved his contempt. He told them, "But God sent me ahead of you to preserve for you a remnant on earth and to save your lives by a great deliverance. So then, it is not you who sent me here, but God. He made me father to Pharaoh, lord of his entire household and ruler of all Egypt."

In other words Joseph's darkest hour and deepest despair were because God Meant It For Good.

Mandi, I don't know what the future holds. Maybe, I'll write something worthwhile. Maybe I'll find that lasting relationship full of love and commitment. All I know is that I have a sense of fullness for the future; where before, life had lost its meaning.

Words will never express my regrets, nor can words express the ordeal that I have endured. Yet, if God is at work in my life, my failings and shortcomings will be used to His good purpose. My failure is His opportunity.

God meant Joseph's ordeal for good. I can only pray that He grant me a fraction of that favor.

The Instinctual Need to Abuse Dad's Stuff

I couldn't help consider the Karmic lesson as I wiped the frosted dew off of my best flashlight. Left out overnight to the mercy of the elements the poor flashlight didn't have a chance against three kids. My first inclination was to get a little upset as I found it mildly disturbing to purchase the same tool more than once. Then, as I remembered my own childhood, I thought, maybe there is some instinctual need for children to abuse a father's possessions.

Reflecting back on my earlier years, I wondered how many times my Dad said, "I don't mind you using my things just take care of them and put them back when you're done."

It's possible that with the correct formula and my Laptop I might be able to compute a number close to how many times he spoke those words. However, what concerned me more was how many times I'd have to say, "I don't mind you using my stuff..." to you guys. My guess is that my earnest plea fell on deaf ears at least nine-hundred-and-sixty-three times.

With my two brothers and I all using Dad's stuff there were many occasions when he'd arrive at his workbench with some project in mind only to spend the first hour of so trying to find his tools. Feeling like he spawned his own personal cast of the Three Stooges, he'd eventually yell, "Hey you guys, get down here." Then, after several minutes of his intense, I don't mind you using my tools lecture, the three of us scurried around the house, yard, and garage retracing our project locations for the last week.

The hammer, saw, and drill lain strewn around the garage where I built a birdhouse. Pliers and wrenches lay in the driveway where Al had been fixing his bike. With Wes searching the yard for screwdrivers that we'd use to play the game mumbly-peg; a sado-macho game consisting of seeing who could throw and stick the screwdriver closest to the other player's foot. Under the strange rules of mumbly-peg, the winner of each round was determined by whose screwdriver was driven in the ground closest to the opposing toes. Not only did you lose the round if you stuck your screwdriver in the opposing toes, but it was consider bad form.

Of course, there were the times when we'd borrow Dad's stuff and have some kind of tragic accident. Like burning up his camping gear (The Camping Trip), or losing his best hunting knife down the hole of an outhouse, or somehow managing to drop his heirloom tackle box over the side of the boat, only to be lost at the bottom of the lake…forever.

Fortunately, as we became older we borrowed Dad's stuff less and less. However, just to let him know that we really care about him, we still borrow some large or expensive tool that we have yet been able to afford. For instance, when I built the dock I needed to borrow his mini chainsaw to rough-cut four-by-six posts. As usual, he graciously lent it to me knowing that nothing ever really changed, and that only a slim chance existed that I would return it in its original condition.

Well, after using up most of the life in his chain saw and failing to get it sharpened, I had to go out and buy my own. Of course, he is welcome to use mine at any time, just so long as he takes care of it and puts it back where it belongs.

Choices

I've often used the expression if you're going to be dumb, you'd better be tough? That's because whoever thought of it had me in mind. Unfortunately, my bad decisions didn't just affect me. I've made so many bad choices that all I can do is thank God that I have the opportunity to make up for some of them.

Have you ever considered the subtle yet powerful forces that influence the decisions we make? Sigmund Freud suggested that there were no accidents. He surmised that somewhere deep in a person's psyche a cause and effect scenario could always be found.

For instance, is it an accident when a man who feels compelled to overwork selects an unsafe ladder, and falls when it crumples beneath him resulting in broken ribs? The outcome is the man is forced to convalesce, spending time to rest and reunite with his family that he felt he'd been neglecting. Was it simply a lack of attention or fatigue, or did he make a decision from some unconscious place deep within his psyche?

Freud would tell us the fall was no accident. The decision to use the ladder was a deeply conscious choice, albeit a bad one.

That does not mean there are not victims. A bad choice by one person is sometimes catastrophic for someone else. I'm not going to go on about driving a car while under the influence of alcohol or drugs, promiscuous sex, or an angry outburst, but I will say that a bad choice can horrifically change lives, and all in a matter of a split second.

Why? Why were we given freewill? What is it about our brain that enables us to contemplate the cosmos, or explore DNA? Other creatures with large brains don't have the complex range of choices that we face. When they hunger they try to eat. When thirsty they seek water. When the season is upon them they mate, and usually at a time so that the gestation period ends when the climate and food source are favorably to the newborn.

So, where did our ability to rationalize and choose come from? And what about the subconscious mind, or the conscience to know right from wrong?

Sixth grade anthropology teaches us that human beings are the new kids on the block, species wise, that is. According to the fossil record, we haven't been around all that long. How did we get such intelligence and awareness so quickly? So far, science has not been able to answer such questions.

The first chapter in Genesis states that the plants came first, possessing only flesh. Next, He made the animals and gave them mind, will, and emotions, or a lesser soul. Last, just like the fossil record shows, the Bible tells us He made man in His own image and: *... breathed into his nostrils the breath of life, and man became a living being.* Genesis 2:7

I believe that not only did God give man a soul, but whatever that breath of life symbolized, God delivered something more into human kind. In that moment, He set us apart from all the rest of creation; He made us spiritual beings. This has become the single most important realization of my existence—that I am both a creature of flesh and blood living in this world, and a creature of spiritual essence belonging in and to the realm of light and God's holiness. Mandi, many people don't get this. I hope and pray that you do, for in choosing to find and accept your spiritual half, you will become whole.

It doesn't require reading the Bible to see that mankind is clearly set apart from the animal kingdom. In fact, we have the responsibility to be stewards of this world, to care for and protect it. To preserve and enlighten, or as Christ said: "To be salt and light."

Genesis goes on to describe the most consequential choice of all mankind: the decision to eat the fruit from the tree of knowledge of good and evil. Which God told Adam and Eve not to do.

But, here's the rub, I've had to ask myself why would an omniscient God who knows what curious fools children are create the circumstances for such a choice? Doesn't it seem inevitable that sooner or later one of us would eat from that tree?

Could it be that was His intention right from the beginning? I personally feel that is the case; mostly because it has been my trials and tribulations that have led me toward a deeper understanding of who He is and the potential that I possess. Even though I carry many regrets, I have learned the most from my mistakes. I'm convinced that without the hardships that I created because of my own bad choices I would only know half of who I am. Without the polarizing effects of evil, what would I really understand of God's goodness? Would I know the happiness and peace that I possess today without the sorrow of my past? Could I truly feel the depth of love, without the need for forgiveness?

I know so little of God's plan, but I do know that freewill carries with it incredible power and consequence. We are creatures of freewill—arguably the loftiest height that consciousness can attain; but to be aware of that dazzling perspective, we must have choices of equal stature. I think it took the tree of knowledge to accomplish that.

At first, I thought the decision was between good and evil; however, I've come to see things slightly different than that simplistic view. I think it's important to realize that the knowledge of good and evil is symbolized in a single fruit of that one tree. The choice was not between a tree of good fruit and a tree of evil fruit. The vital choice was between the tree of knowledge or the second tree, the tree of life—specifically spiritual life. A life united with God. Doesn't it stands to reason that by choosing to live a spirit-led life, a life directed by God, that right decisions would follow. This doesn't mean life will be easy. The lives depicted in the Bible show us that. Nevertheless, I'm convinced that the changes in the heart that occur for those who finally choose the fruit that draws a person closer to God will automatically lead a person toward a life of good decisions, and so much more.

Remember, the tree of knowledge is about worldly things. Even making the choice to do all the good humanly possibly will not direct a person to his or her ultimate divine destiny. Only by choosing the tree of life will we attain the goal God has set before us.

How do you choose the tree of life?

I believe that Christ is that choice.

His life gave each of us that second chance. He returned the choice to us to either pursue the outward realm of physical experience and earthly knowledge, or to turn one's journey inward and transcend the ego in order to connect with the great I Am. He even showed us how.

Choosing the tree of life is choosing to be led by your spirit, your inner heart, something whose roots go even deeper than your unconscious mind. The only other choice is to let your mind, will, and emotions, or your soul, lead you through this life. Unfortunately, that part of who you are, your mind, will, and emotions, is foreign to the spiritual realm. By depending solely on your mind and emotions to guide you, you'll be restricted to this world. The alarming thing then becomes who the Bible tells us has dominion over this earthly realm, and who can influence our minds and emotions. The Bible tells us that when satan was cast out of heaven he was sent here and given reign over this natural world. If you experience life only on the conscious and emotional level you'll be ignoring your spiritual side, the half of you connected to God and His guidance. As long as we perceive things with only our physical abilities, we are playing on satan's home turf--turf upon which we can never win.

The drama played out by Adam, Eve, and the serpent, represented the final stage in becoming human. Which means they were given the awesome responsibility of determining their own destiny. God placed in Adam and Eve the incredible power of freewill, at the same time creating in them the traits of wonderment and curiosity, and the craving for new experiences.

Why would He do that?

Could it be that it's the trials of life that separate the wheat from the tares? That without the knowledge of good and evil we would be mindless servants, blindly following His will? Could it be that it's a person's trials and tribulations, and yes, even a person's mistakes that have the potential to lead him closer to God? Could it be the consequences of those choices that end up pushing him into God's consuming fire in order to be cleansed of pridefulness and self-reliance. Could it be the obstacles (sin) that we create in this material world that leads us to look for solutions in the spiritual? Then, in that moment of divine cleansing, as God's fire burns away the dross of the ego, the eyes of his heart open. And that person begins to comprehend the unseen world of the spiritual realm.

I believe that's part of the reason why we're here. I'm talking about the actual meaning of life stuff. I believe we're here to be educated, tested, and awakened spiritually. Our divine destiny for those who choose it is to become sons and daughters of the light, but with that comes incredible responsibility. Each of us has been created to be spiritual heirs destined to inherit the wonders of the universe. But each of us must prove that he or she can be trusted; that we finally get it. So, each of us is required to make that ultimate decision—to either turn toward God or away from Him. To be led by our spirit or by our soul.

The true wonder is that God in His loving pursuit of each of us can turn even our worst mistakes and bad choices into opportunities for spiritual growth. Mandi, I know this to be true. Without my mistakes, I don't think I would have ever seen past my ego, and I would never have found the God I have come to know and love. I would have finished this life unfulfilled and half alive. And only God knows what awaited me then.

I'm reminded of two passages: *For God is a consuming fire.* *Hebrews* 12:29 And, *My grace is sufficient for you, my power is made perfect in weakness.* 2 Corinthians 12:9

Mandi, it's all about the choices. Choose love.

The Road of Pain and Fear

I don't believe it is possible to journey through this life and at some point not be faced with devastating circumstances or life threatening realities. As shattering and life changing as those times can be, I now understand the opportunity that is created. If cared for in courage and spiritual compliance, it is during such times when a person can embark on a soulful inward journey that begins when each of us, sooner or later, find ourselves standing at the crossroads named Life and Eternity.

I have stood at this crossroad. If you'll walk with me, metaphorically that is, I'll show you what I've learned.

If we travel ahead in the direction the mind wants to go, we will continue on the road of Life. Having traveled this way most of mine, I've come to know it by its other name: the path of pride. If we choose that way we will continue to believe the illusion that we are in total control. Unfortunately, that perspective also keeps us from connecting to the inner consciousness that lives a subtle existence below the ego that maintains that view. As long as we look at the world through the mask of self-image, we will never truly understand the kingdom of God that exists within.

You and I are going to venture forward on the other road named Eternity. When we begin this trip you'll find it to be the hardest and most grievous thing you have ever done. And many have come to know this part of the journey as the road of Pain and Fear.

How well I know those first steps. They are the most excruciating you will ever take. But I have been down this road, and if, when the time comes you make the right choice, I promise you that it will be worthwhile.

The road of Pain and Fear is a spiritual pathway. And I have found that it is only open once or twice in a lifetime. You'll recognize it because the first steps are filled with more emotional and/or physical pain than you think you can bear. I now how alone you'll feel as you stumble under the intensity of you burden, and if I could, I would help you carry it, but I can't. Right now there are no short cuts, no detours. There are only suffering and tears. As tortuous as it may seem, the pain is necessary; it is God's furnace of spiritual reclamation. You see, this journey transcends the physical world and enters into the spiritual realm where you require different senses to experience it. Facing your pain is for many the baptism of fire that is the beginning of a new life in which the eyes of the heart are opened. ...*He will baptize you with the Holy Spirit and with fire.* Luke 3:16

Can you feel your ego being stripped away?

You must decrease so the He can increase.

Can you feel who you are crumbling to ashes?

You, the ego part of you, must die.

As hard as it is to believe right now, the anxiety that feels like an unquenchable fire burning in your heart can become the most sacred thing in your life. If you let it, that searing pain will open your soul to self-examination and God's righteous judgment.

You will see the mistakes you have made with never before seen clarity.

You will understand the affect you have had on others? You'll begin to see how your selfishness has kept you from who your truly are.

Then, as the flames melt your ego, the eyes of your heart will begin to open. You'll soon be able to comprehend things that you have never before known.

Look over there. Can you see that billboard?

It reads, *I have come to bring fire to the earth, and how I wish it were burning already.* Luke 12:49

Pain can fuel that spiritual fire, and Christ knew that without it total repentance is difficult if not impossible to achieve. Until we truly face our sins and iniquities with a broken and contrite heart, we cannot fully repent and give them to Christ in order to receive His blessed relief.

The road of Pain and Fear is leading you to the gates of consciousness, melting your false self-image, and allowing your corruption and impurities to rise to the surface of awareness where they can be recognized and released.

The gates of consciousness are just ahead. Can you see the warning? Let me read it for you: *Enter by the narrow gate. For wide is the gate and broad is the road that leads to destruction, and many enter through it. But small is the gate and narrow the road that leads to life, and only a few find it.* Matthew 7:13-14 (NIV)

Your pain and fear has led you to the narrow gate. Push the latch and open it so that we may enter.

It's locked?

Oh, that's right. This is where you must make a decision. If you choose to remain who you were, giving control back to your ego centered in self, you will end up back in the illusion of the life you had, and this gate will remain locked. Only the wide gate will be open to you. The other choice is to let Christ into your heart replacing who you are with who He is.

Can you see the inscription above the lock?

Except a man (or woman) be born again, he cannot see the kingdom of God. John 3:3

If you look very closely, you'll see a second inscription. I know it by heart.

I am the gate, by me if any man enter in he shall be saved and shall go in and out, and find pasture. John 10:9

Here, let me open it so that we may continue. Just remember that you will have to make a choice if you wish to return.

By the way, did you notice the road signs?

The name of the road going through the wide gate was Sin and Grief. Ultimately the wide road will always lead you there. Now look at the sign for the narrow road.

That's right, Comfort and Peace.

F. Edward Marx   To Mandi, with Love

You see how easy the decision becomes once you truly let Him in? I personally have had enough sin and grief to last a lifetime. Let's continue down the path of Comfort and Peace.

Why don't we stop here for a minute at Isaiah 41:40. *So do not fear, for I am with you; do not be dismayed, for I am your God. I will strengthen you and help you. I will uphold you with my righteous right hand.*

Now, I will ask you to trust me, for my own life has proven Romans 8:28 to be true. *And we know that in all things God works for the good of those who love Him, who have been called according to His purpose.*

I promise you that no matter how dark it may seem, God can make something good happen and bring a new light into your life-- if you let Him.

Just a little farther and we can rest at Psalm 23:1-4.
The Lord is my Shepard, I shall not want.
He maketh me lie down in green pasture;
He leadeth me beside still waters.
He restoreth my soul:
He leadeth me in the path of righteousness for His namesake.
Yea, I walk through the valley of the shadow of death I will fear no evil:
For Thou art with my:
Thy rod and staff, they comfort me.

Unfortunately, I can take you no further. It is time for you to continue ahead on your own. You are approaching the intersection of Faith. While you may have journeyed on this road before, you have never had the opportunity to go this far. The road that began in Pain and Fear is one of the shortest routes to Faith, and it can take you farther than you have ever gone before.

Each step that you take on the road of Faith that is not filtered and distorted by your ego will draw you closer to Christ. As you decrease so that He may increase, you will never be alone—no matter what road you find yourself traveling.

F. Edward Marx   To Mandi, with Love

   Look there is someone up ahead. Can you hear Him calling? I can. He's saying, "Come unto me all ye who labor and are heavy laden, and I will give you rest."

The Camping Trip

The summer before my junior year in high school was nearly half over and so far not a single catastrophe worth remembering had occurred. Not considered an adult, yet no longer a kid, the days dragged by in summer vacation purgatory. But the worst thing of all was that I still couldn't drive.

One long lazy August day, my buddy Ken and I convinced ourselves that we were dying of boredom. So we came up with the grand plan of taking a nice long camping and canoe trip. Ken's older brother reluctantly let us use his canoe. Then, after utilizing every psychological trick at my 15-year-old command, I convinced my Dad with the logic of: What could happen on a simple camping trip? So he let me take his tent, sleeping bag, fishing equipment, including his best rod and reel. Ken snatched his brother's camping stove, sleeping bag, and cooler.

I didn't know it at the time, but this was to be my initial lesson in the value of using someone else's stuff, thereby keeping my own equipment in reserve. While we planned on living off the land, we also took a hundred pounds of food as an emergency back up.

Ken's brother drove us to our launching site on a large group of lakes connected by navigable streams. Then with an intrepid wave goodbye, he said, "Be careful. Have a good time, and I'll see you back here in a week." Then as an afterthought he added, "Hey! Isn't that my stove? That's my cooler! Who said you could use my sleeping bag?" After a quick wave, we paddled just a little faster pretending not hear.

One of the first things that got our attention was the two tiny inches of the canoe's sidewalls that remained above the water line. The wave from a falling leaf would have been big enough to swamp us. Yet, adventure waited, so we dauntingly sliced through the water with only those two measly inches separating us from a waterlogged disaster.

F. Edward Marx   To Mandi, with Love

The first thought that comes to mind is that we would have tipped the canoe over and ended our trip before it began. But that never happened; the fates had far more exciting things in store for us. Just tipping over with most of our gear sinking to the bottom of the lake, or floating away, would have been much to usual and mundane for the fates that challenge and govern my life.

After several hours of paddling, we spied a grassy peninsula with a little knoll that overlooked the lake. Then, almost as a celestial beacon, a patch of golden sunlight broke through the clouds highlighting a perfect camping spot.

Well, it was almost perfect. After setting up camp, it dawned on us just how grassy the knoll turned out to be. The grass stood so tall that the only time we could see anything was when we stood up. After the first day, we came to the conclusion that this just wasn't good enough. Who wanted to sit around on a beautiful lake only to see as far as the grass in front of our faces? Certainly, not us. So we came up with a plan. One of us had recently seen a film about rainforest farmers using fire to clear an area. It made perfect sense that if farmers could do such a thing, we could certainly clear a small patch without any problem. So we carefully lit a small little brush fire and let it burn a few square yards of the tallest grass in front of our tent. After putting the fire out, we looked things over, and Ken said, "Hey that's great, that really worked well."

It worked so well and was such a simple task that we decided to clear a larger section down to where the canoe was tied to a tree. The idea being that we would have a clear view of the lake. After a little planning we lit a second fire. Steering the fire by stomping out wayward flames we leisurely burned unwanted grass.

Suddenly, the wind kicked up. I'm convinced the fates needed a chuckle as they fanned our little fire into a blaze that we could no longer stomp out. Feeding on dry grass and a stiff hot breeze our small blaze roared to life. Almost instantly, it began to burn a lot more acreage then planned. In a matter of a minute or two, we went from a calm carefree mood to one of shear panic and terror with fire burning all around us. We both ran to the tent and grabbed our borrowed sleeping bags. Then, we ran down to the lake, soaked the sleeping bags, and began putting out the fire by throwing the wet bags on the rising flames. A couple of seconds later that spot would be extinguished so we could move our smoldering bags a few feet over onto the next portion of the blaze. When the bags dried out or were to hot to hold, we dragged them back to the lake resoaking them. Once they were good and heavy, we'd run back to the fire and start the exhaustive process all over again.

The one thing that probably saved us from making the headlines along with our parents having to hire a team of lawyers was that we were on the end of the peninsula. By concentrating our efforts at putting out the fire-line heading up the hill, which by the way, connected our private little forest fire to the rest of the world, we could let the remaining fire burn itself out as it hit the edges of the lake.

After hours of exhaustive, hot, smoke and terror filled effort, not to mention searing our fingertips with steaming hot sleeping bags, we finally dragged the last of the flames out.

Returning to the smoldering remains of our campsite, collapsing in the ashes, I notice that we had a really nice panoramic view of the lake. I also notice that all of our camping gear including the tent lay in ashes. My Dad's expensive rod and reel was just a twisted blob of melted plastic and metal leaning against the charred remnants of the blackened cooler. And our fire-blanket-sleeping-bags were nothing more than burnt pieces of tattered cloth.

Eventually, I looked over at Ken who sat with his head between his knees and said, "Breaking camp and packing up won't be too hard, just grab the tent stakes and we can leave whenever you're ready."

Sitting there recuperating while dipping my tortured fingertips into the cool water of the lake, I came to a life realization. If you're going to be dumb, you've got to be tough.

F. Edward Marx   To Mandi, with Love

The Prisons of Life

I used to think of prisons strictly in the context of concrete and steel bars, but that perspective has changed. Prisons come in many forms some physical some psychological, but whatever the type of bondage that occurs is, it is no less effective in holding captive a person's mind, body, or soul.

Even with the world as my toy box, I now realize freedom was only a mirage. Sure I could work as hard as I pleased while entertaining my heart's desires; but even in such liberties the subconscious chains of resentment and stress formed psychological shackles that imprisoned my heart and mind.

It hardly seems to matter the nature of the distress, marital unfulfillment, a failing job, overdue bills, low self-esteem, loneliness, or depression; they all serve to insidiously capture a person's psyche. Then for escape, many--including myself--have sought relief in mood-altering abuses with the most common being alcohol, drugs, sex, gambling, and food. Even something as harmless as shopping can become addictive if it becomes a mood-altering activity. Unfortunately, the momentary relief that is achieved is no more than a chemical illusion in the brain based in the self-deception of being able to temporarily cast aside the stresses of life. Eventually, the repeated attempts to seek relief lead directly to the prisons of: addiction, disease, or obesity, as well as, family and financial problems.

By not understanding the despondent spiral of codependency, I expended a great deal of energy trying to care for and please those around me. Unfortunately, I failed to recognize the need to care also for myself. Despairingly, I found myself trapped in a life that I could no longer sustain or control. Since I neither had God or the ability to honestly self-examine my situation, I fell into the desperate captivity of denying what was wrong and suppressing how I felt. This left my subconscious feeling trapped in the circumstances that I had created, yet instinctively needed to escape.

Eventually, my personal demons of stress and unfulfillment formed the bondage from which I sought relief, and that was all the excuse I needed to engage in the mood-altering activities that led to addiction.

It took God to sit me still long enough to open my eyes to what gambling, drugs, sex, overeating or drinking were all about. My behavior had one purpose, that being to offer escape from myself, along with the issues of day-to-day reality that I did not want to face.

Could there be a more ineffective effort then to try to escape from one's self? Yet, as a society, we spend billions of so called recreational dollars and immeasurable hours on the effort. With the only lasting accomplishment being the addictive tightening of the binge then remorse cycle.

In the spirituality that I have found I am no longer compelled to work sixty to seventy hours per week, nor do I hunger for material things. I won't let myself order a large, double cheese and pepperoni pizza as my good health and fitness are far too important to me. Nor do I even desire to go to a bar to try to find some equally inebriated woman for an escape into a candle-lit realm full of the hazards of sexual disease, AID's, unwanted pregnancy, or just plain guilt over the degradation of my soul.

What I am free to do, as we all are, is to contemplate spiritual matters, which I have found to be immensely satisfying. I didn't realize it, but I longed to grow close to God all my life. There was something missing that only He could fill. And through some miracle of spiritually infused honest self-examination, I can now delve deeply into my own psychology. I am finally gaining the understanding of who I am, and what I must do in order to fill the spiritual void I felt all my life. I have also gained a focused sense of destiny. I know why I am here and what I am supposed to do.

Like the Phoenix, I am rising out of my ashes of self-destruction. Never again will I live in my ego's illusion of control—

F. Edward Marx   To Mandi, with Love

too proud to seek professional help or ministerial counseling. I
realized that in my self-deluding arrogance I believed I was in total
control. Without even knowing it, I let life continue to close in on me,
tighter and tighter, until I could no longer psychologically accept the
restraint. Unfortunately, when my unconscious mind found the
strategy that would facilitate my release, it also shattered every last one
of the hearts that loved and cared for me.

I've learned that in many ways psychology is a game of
opposites. There is no surer way to have unfulfilled needs manifest in
some destructive manner than to suppress them. By seeking mood-
altering activities to try to escape my difficult emotions, the more
negative my feelings became. The more I ignored or suppressed my
growing unfulfillment, the more the mood-altering-addictive-grip
tightened. Which at age forty-four only served to separate me farther
from my then impatient destiny.

I found no lasting escape in mood-altering activities. The path
to freedom lie not away from my problems, or relief from who I was;
paradoxically, I found my freedom by embracing the negative aspect of
life (my sin) and facing what I feared. Only when I turned on the light
of truthful self-examination and descended the corridors of personal
responsibilities into my darkest mental dungeons did I begin my
journey on the ascending stairs of personal enlightenment.

I achieved my freedom by first accepting and recognizing the
bondage that I had allowed to entrap me. Then, by directing my
attention toward the arcane source of my distress, I found the
connective tendrils linking me to my sinful past. Eventually, I was
able to discover the roots responsible for holding me emotionally
captive. Then, in heart-wrenching repentance, I began to sever the
hold that ultimately freed me from the stifling prison of self.

Imprisonment comes in many forms, with one type of
psychological bondage often leading to another. Yet, there is freedom
for each and every one of us if we come to the point of realizing that
we need help, especially spiritual help. I could feel the mood-altering
bars forming around me, yet I choose to ignore them. Deep within I

could feel the destroyers grip tightening around my soul, but I did nothing to stop it. I didn't want to face my mistakes, or figure out what to do about them. I wasn't strong enough. My weakness of pride and arrogance became the cataclysmic defect that brought about the destruction of who I was and the family that I loved.

For what my nightmarish journey through a labyrinth of pain is worth, it wasn't until I found the courage to begin caring for my soul that my mind gained its freedom. Now my liberation of consciousness transcends far beyond this physical realm. I am truly free.

The Trials and Tribulations of Exotic Foods

My dilemma with exotic foods began at a early age when I bought into my mother's philosophy of, "I don't care if you eat it, just try it to see if you like it, otherwise how will you ever know." This unfortunately made sense to me and I have suffered the consequences in gastronomical adventures ever since.

Having learned that Brussels sprouts weren't so bad and that strange looking foods like Lobster and Shrimp were delicious, I developed the mistaken impression that most of the new foods I tried, would turn out to be a pleasant experience.

The culinary aspect of my diet really began to change when I lived in Hawaii. With great anticipation, I looked forward to attending an authentic wedding Luau in celebration of my Hawaiian friend, Derek, sister's marriage. He promised an all you could eat, and then some, Hawaiian buffet. Then he invited me to participate in preparing and cooking Ka-lua pig. Which is really just a pre-party the night before the real party in which the pig is steamed under ground in a sand pit, lined with layers of red-hot lava rocks.

The pig, encased in all it's Hawaiian wrappings is laid on top of the lava rocks and covered with shredded banana tree stumps, Ti leaves, and finally sand. This effectively formed a giant ocean-front pressure cooker that rendered two-hundred-and-fifty pounds of pork into a mouth watering delicacy.

Once the pig was in place and roasting there was not much to do for the next ten to twelve hours. It seemed that the main past time was to sit around drinking beer, listening to the waves, and "talking story".

After an ear full of story talk someone realized he was hungry and brought up the topic of food. Instantly, we were all starving and the cry went out, "Lets get something to eat."

Thinking this a good idea, I gathered myself together for a trip into town wondering if any stores would be open this late. Off we trundled to the cars, but instead of getting in and driving away, every body just grabbed buckets and flashlights, with one guy retrieving his fishing pole and tackle. Then without any sign of communication that I could detect, everyone headed back toward the beach. Momentarily dazed and confused, as I know I didn't see a Taco Hut back there, I followed everyone like a little lost puppy. Derek in his usual good nature, merrily handed me a bucket and flashlight and said, "Come on, lets go find something to eat." Of course, I didn't realize at the time that the operative word here was thing. Which Derek pronounced ting.

Heading back toward the rocks and the ocean, the first chore Derek completed was burying his five-gallon bucket even with the top of the sand, just above the high tide mark. This created a round, fourteen-inch-deep pit. Derek then produced a piece of pork fat, threw it into the bucket and told me that the sand crabs will smell the pork, walk up to the edge of the bucket and fall in.

Wondering what that had to do with food, I went along with this strange behavior.

Next we walked to the edge of the ocean where the waves broke onto the rocks. Derek handed me his flashlight and said, "You hold the light, and I'll get em."

"Get what?" I asked as I looked around only to see barren rocks, sand, and breaking waves. Beginning to question my friends grip on sanity, or at least the amount of beer he drank, I watched him as he peered into crevasses, and turned over rocks. Then as if greeting some long lost pet he exclaimed, "There you are." Pulling out his small knife, he pried off the miniature tee-pee shaped, half dollar sized shells that tenaciously clung to the black lava rock. He also threw into the bucket some black, and purple, spiny sea urchins. Adding the comment, "The purple ones are a lot better than the black ones."

From my perspective, neither of them looked any good. Aside from trying to eat what looked like a medieval instrument of torture, I figured starvation was the first and only course on the menu tonight. We finally gathered a generous portion of Opehii (pronounced O-pee-hee) and Sea Urchins, more than enough in my opinion. Then we strolled back to check on our sand crab trap.

Shinning the light into the bottom of the bucket, I spied about thirty crabs, three to five inches long (mostly legs) scrambling around in the bottom of the bucket. With a satisfied grunt Derek said, "Good," grabbed the bucket and we returned to our makeshift kitchen complete with campfire.

Looking at the spindly, scrambling, crustaceans, I still had no idea what they could be for. My best guess was they might be bait for the guy with the fishing pole, but he'd already caught three nice sized fish. Then, when he filleted his catch into strips about the sized of my little finger, I thought maybe that was bait. The whole thing was getting more and more confusing.

I watched in a somewhat terrified yet fascinated trance as my Hawaiian friends prepared our little repast. The Opehii were boiled in ocean water, the sea urchins were cracked open and along with the fish served raw. And the piesta d'resistance, the sand crabs, were thrown into a pot of boiling oil and French-fried. At least that mystery was solved, for a while I had visions of trying to wrestle a live crab into my mouth as it anchored itself to my lip clinging on for dear life.

The Opehii turned out to be pretty good, similar to steamed mussels. Since this was my first experience with raw fish, I was pleasantly surprised, and have come to acquire a taste for "Shusi." The sea urchins had the consistency of loose Jell-O and tasted like iodine, not a combination that I can heartily recommend (and that was a purple one). The French-fried sand crabs, eaten in their entirety, tasted like a potato chip with legs, stuffed with crab dip. Thanks to the case of beer I sucked down in the process, it wasn't all that bad.

Next came my stint in the Philippines with barbecue meat on a stick a local favorite. When I asked the vendor what kind of meat it was, there was always only one answer—beef, however, some of it really didn't taste like beef. And after living there for several months, I learned that beef could be cat, dog, pork or even monkey.

With all the strange foods that I ate in the Philippines, there was no food more "exotic" than a Baloot. A Baloot is a fertile duck or chicken egg left under the hen for seven days. Then it's buried in the sand for another two weeks. You eat a Baloot like a hard boiled egg, with a good Baloot tasting like its been dipped in chicken soup. A bad Baloot is crunchy.

Tim and I grabbed a jeepney to return from a late night excursion in the Barrio. It was sort of like grabbing a taxi that looked more like a pickup truck. We paid our fifty centavos and hopped into the back. One of our fellow passengers was a Baloot man. He was called the Baloot man because every morning just after dawn, he walked through the streets of the sleeping city hollering at the top of his lungs--Baa...looooot. Before I knew what a Baloot was, I thought this guy was the town's official alarm clock calling out to the sleeping city that it was Baloot o'clock and time to get up.

Hanging on as the Jeepney bounced along, the Baloot man held up an egg and asked Tim or I if we wanted one.

We readily declined, however the Baloot man persisted somehow calling our manhood into question. Well, a dare is a dare, and since we both drank the prerequisite keg of beer, which by the way was the only thing one can do to find enough fortitude to choke down a Baloot, we finally gave in. After several minutes of bickering we negotiated a satisfactory price. Actually, I tried to pay the Baloot man off instead of eating the thing, but Tim would have none of that. We peeled the shells of our questionable eggs, and in one big mouthful popped them in. My Baloot wasn't too bad. I managed to get it down with only a minor digestive rebellion. Tim, unfortunately, had a bad Baloot. As I am heard him crunch through the tiny not yet developed bones along with the differing shades of his complexion, I knew that the final score was going to be Baloot one, Tim zero. Fortunately, Jeepney's are open air vehicles, so when Tim turned, stuck his green head out of the side and lost his cookies, it didn't cause much of a problem.

Of course, like any good salesman, the Baloot man wanted to compensate Tim for his less than agreeable dining experience. While he didn't actually offer Tim his money back, he did tell him he could have another Baloot.

During my first business trip to Japan, I accepted a dinner invitation. It's customary to treat a special guest to an expensive Japanese restaurant specializing in exotic sushi, as if regular sushi wasn't exotic enough. The other thing that this restaurant was noted for was its "fresh" seafood. Which in the context of a Japanese restaurant can also be described in other terms, like still moving when it's set down in front of you.

Through the courses of dinner all these new and strange foods would appear in front of me. Being the polite guest, not to mention that each dish probably cost about the same as the family's grocery bill for the week, I tried to eat everything that they placed in front of me. Which I didn't realize at the time was turning into a game for my hosts called: Let's see if there is anything he won't eat.

The evening progressed well, with each of us drinking a copious amount of hot Sake. As we joked and laughed while having a marvelous time, our chef placed a whole shrimp, minus the shell off its tail on each of our plates. Then, in his best English, he said, "Verdy fresh."

I looked over to my hosts and watched as they pulled the raw shrimp tail from its body. When they dipped it into some special black sauce and popped the whole thing in their mouths, I followed suit. As I put the shrimp's half-eaten carcass back down on my plate, I noticed a slight movement in one of its antennae. Fascinated by the shrimp's twitching, I continued to watch as it gathered itself together, stood up and tried to walk away.

Well, my hosts thought this was great stuff with comments like, "See we told you, the freshest seafood in town. It just doesn't get any fresher than that."

I politely chuckled as I watched my half eaten dinner trying to make its exit, stage left.

Somehow our conversation shifted to Blow fish sushi, or fugu. Which if not prepared perfectly by a well-trained chef will kill the person eating it. I had to excuse myself for a few minutes and when I returned, I noticed a different cup of hot Sake at my place. Lifting it to propose a toast, I spied a brown, crusty, fish fin lying at the bottom of my cup. As I inquired about this new item in my Sake, my host looked at me and said, "It's Blow fish fin."

I asked, "What is it for?"

Trying to remain straight-faced and serious, my host could contain his mirth no longer as he blurted out, "It takes the poison out of the Sake, ha ha ha."

F. Edward Marx   To Mandi, with Love

The Slight Genetic Defect In Men

I have a theory as to why men behave so badly when it comes time to make a commitment and nurture a monogamous relationship. My theory is that a small yet undiscovered defect exists in a man's genes. Not to be confused with the small mind of it's own defect in his jeans. Once this gene is discovered there should be a collective apology from all the women of the world, as it will then be understood that we could not help ourselves. Until then, I can only offer anecdotal evidence of its existence through the following story.

Looking back through the lens of time, prior to any recording of the ways of mankind, our ancestor's eked out a small existence by hunting, gathering, and scavenging. With the women of that time providing the same primary role of mother, nurturer, and keeper of the hearth as they still do today. Men, on the other hand, had to wander, following the herds or scouting out a new cave for the tribe to spend the winter in. In general, the tribe's survival meant that men were required to be "out there" looking for the greener grass.

During this early era in man's developmental stages, the like-to-roam, or curiosity gene, was not very well developed. Not many people know that it just so happened to be mutating in one of our early ancestors. Who at sixteen, had reached the venerable status of middle age. Upon this milestone the tribe's right of passage required that he go out and bring something of value back. So along with his boyhood friend, these two young men named Ew and Ah ventured forth.

Since names weren't that common in those days, it usually took some special event or circumstances to actually have a sound associated with one's person. Unfortunately, Ew first heard his name as a young boy after being sprayed by a huge prehistoric skunk. Then the name stuck because whenever he got wet or began to sweat, the smell would reactivate to its original potency and everyone would hold their noses and say, "Ewww".

Ah, on the other hand was a handsome lad. Remarkably all his teeth were still intact, and his forehead was less pronounced, so the young girls always smiled at him and grunted an agreeable, "Ahhhh", as he shyly looked away.

Having left their home cave far behind our two intrepid wanderers ventured upon another tribe of prehistoric people. This first contact was always a touchy situation since Ew and Ah were never sure if they would be invited for dinner, or end up as dinner. In this case they were lucky, the Smith clan was friendly.

After dinner when all the local news had been exchanged, Mr. Smith got an idea. He had lately noticed that all the little Smiths, while they look a lot like him, seemed a little funny. Mr. Smith figured something was not quite right. He had a sneaking suspicion that there just weren't enough Smith men to go around. So, after Ew and Ah settled in for the night, he sent the Smith girls into the boys' furs. Of course, Ah got most of the attention.

The rest is natural history. From that day on, Ah traveled the land sowing his wild oats, including the like-to-roam-gene now fully developed.

As it turned out, that like-to-roam-gene was one of those beneficial adaptations that Darwin was so keen on. The men who like to roam became better hunters as they gained more experience and covered wider territories. They also provided other tribes with a larger gene pool while spreading the knowledge of tools and crafts that they had acquired along their journeys.

Now, after a few million years of men liking to roam, civilization has changed our society from hunters and gatherers to farmers, doctors, and plumbers. The problem, as I see it, is that a few thousand years of civilization does not remove the genetic aspect of man's development. Women, who have been living the same role all along, all of a sudden expect men to stay home, especially since they figured out that the hunting and gathering thing is called the supermarket. Subsequently, men are required to change, practically overnight in beneficial adaptation terms. Unfortunately, women have no concept of how hard it is to turn off that simple little genetic predisposition and remove the compulsion to roam and sow a few wild oats.

I don't know about the rest of the men out there, but I know I'm trying. It's just not that easy to overcome a few million years of genetically instilled behavior.

The Real Cost of Hunting and Fishing

I always gained a certain satisfaction out of feeding my friends and family a freshly caught fish dinner, or a finely seasoned baked pheasant or grouse, and especially a delicious slow cooked elk or venison pot roast. Invariably, when the meal concludes, someone mentions, "That was delicious, and it really didn't cost you anything, did it?"

At that point I just smile while I run through the calculations of the total cost of that piece of Alaskan King salmon. My mental audit goes something like this: Heavy duty fishing gear $350.00, plane fare to Alaska $750.00, plane fare to Kodiak Island $250.00, float plane trip into the interior of Kodiak Island $325.00, cabin rental $500.00, fish processing and dry ice packaging $150.00, miscellaneous supplies $250.00. Total price of the 50 pounds of frozen salmon I lugged through airports, $2575.00 or $51.50 per pound.

It was my Uncle Ed who first taught me how to properly calculate the true cost of hunting and fishing. He belonged to a hunt club whose membership fee, back in the sixties was $2500.00. His annual dues were $500.00. His hunting outfit, fully accessories, topped out at about $250. His brand new shotgun $650.00, shells $20.00, and each pheasant bagged was $5.50 a bird not including the $1.50 cleaning fee. After the first day of hunting with 10 birds in the bag, Uncle Ed said to me, "I hope your aunt really likes pheasant, but just between you and me, let's not tell her they work out to $396.55 a bird."

For years I have deer hunted with Mac, and Mitch, mostly for the camaraderie and friendship. With each of us looking forward to the annual ritual. Deer are beautiful animals and I don't know if I can ever shoot another, however, being out in the Northern Michigan woods watching them with my two life-long buddies is certainly near the top of my yearly agenda. When I did bring down one of those animals, I justified it with the rationale that there is an overpopulation crisis in the deer herd and the thinning of the herd is important to maintaining it's over all health. Plus my family is fond of Venison with nothing going to waste.

A few years ago I bagged a magnificent eight-point buck. His thick evenly matched antlers were the trophy I'd hunted. However, if I add up the money I spent over the years I'd been hunting, I calculated that it worked out to be about $3,476.37 per rump roast.

Mitch learned a fairly traumatic lesson in the real cost of hunting and fishing. One of the very first times Mitch fished with Mac and I, he caught a beautiful five-pound Bass. The thrill of landing that fairy tale fish so enthralled him that within six months he purchased all of the equipment he could possibly need, including a brand new 150 horse Bass boat.   Apparently, Mitch read somewhere that any respectable Bass fisherman, worth his Rapella, must arrive quickly and be able to keep up with those really speedy fish. The trauma of all this is that Mitch has never caught another nice Bass, and since you can't really count the first one, the score is Mitch 0, Bass $15,879.00

Mac, who owns (is paying for) the property that Mitch and I allow him to invite us to every year, has the added perspective of a mortgage payment and taxes to calculate in his cost. For Mac, this pretty much puts the cost of hunting and fishing into the category of, I'd rather not think about it.

So, if you're ever invited over to a wild game dinner, consider that you could be sipping champagne, and dinning on caviar and filet mignon--in Paris--for what your host has spent for that morsel on your plate.

F. Edward Marx   To Mandi, with Love

Journal of a Fishing Expedition

July 28th

4:30 pm	Purchased all species fishing license. I haven't fished for all species in my entire life, this could be the year. Purchased new tackle and lures. My hundred-odd-pounds of old tackle and lures, accumulated from other fishing expedition, is somehow not adequate. Besides, I now realize it is not about catching fish, it's about keeping the economy stimulated--stimulation rate $48.78.
5:03 pm	Explained to Mac that by the time I help pay for gas and bait, buy the cooler full of expedition necessities such as soda, candy bars, and potato chips, that the ten pounds of Walleye I plan on catching should only cost a reasonable $10.00 a pound. This could possible be the most inexpensive fishing expedition on record.
8:35 pm	Called Carol and promised her a delicious freshly caught Walleye dinner. Yum….

July 29th day of expedition

1:35 am	Woke filled with anticipation and an even fuller bladder.
1:45 am	Still awake—vision of hungry Walleye dancing in my head.
1:47 am	Looked at clock.
1:49 am	Clock still running.
2:05 am	Almost fell back to sleep, but specks of dust settling around me disturbed my restfulness.
2:30 am	Decided to get up. Fishing expeditions are best begun before dawn.
3:00 am	Not leaving for another hour, might as well write Carol a letter explaining how wonderful I am--for

	some reason she seems to be having trouble figuring this out.
4:05 am	Truck's loaded, Mac and Mitch are waiting, time to go.
4:10 am	Gas tank's filled, coffee cup's full, country and western music playing. I think I hit the mother-load.
6:32 am	Mitch can't find the boat launch. Suspects someone has moved it.
6:35 am	Normally asking for direction is out of the question, but when you're burning up prime fishing time emergency tactics are in order. Pulled into 24-hour Coney Island.
6:45 am	Find boat launch, Mitch relieved to know that whoever stole the boat launch only moved it one street over.
7:00 am	On the water, beautiful day, hooking up, only one minor problem--boat running poorly. Mitch slightly concerned. Having owned several boats myself, it is times like this that help remind me why I no longer keep a watercraft.
7:15 am	Five minutes without a bite, time to move.
7:16 am	Boat running poorer still, current strong, could end up in Lake Erie.
7:20 am	Decide to pull into marina to look at sick engine, maybe find new spark plugs.
7:30 am	Marina closed. Mitch inspects spark plugs, no joy.
8:00 am	Decided to leave marina, but sick engine will not engage gears.
8:01 am	Dead in the water, fishing forecast looks poor.
8:10 am	Begin paddling back to boat launch.
8:30 am	Finally reach the exit of the marina, one paddle turns out not be the most effective means of propulsion.
8:31 am	Get to add the Detroit River to my list of canoe trips.
8:45 am	Shoreline bystander sees us paddling and comments, "Lost your prop, hey."

Mitch replied, "No, we have other problems."

Shoreline bystander points to outdrive that has been raised out the water.

Inspection of lower unit reveals that brand new propeller is actually missing.

Look on Mitch's face is cause for concern and helps me vanquish any pleasant thoughts about boat ownership. I believe Mitch's heart to be strong enough. He should recover.

8:47 am   Fishing forecast looks very poor.

9:30 am   Return to boat launch.

9:31 am   Mitch calculates repair cost at slightly over four hundred dollars. Another typical fishing expedition is complete.

9:32 am   Begin looking forward to the next fishing expedition.

Beyond Coincidence

I no longer believe in coincidence. My personal experience has convinced me that there is an unseen, and poorly understood spiritual world that has tremendous effect on our daily lives.

These influences aren't that difficult to recognize, they are based in either love or fear, but they have an uncanny way of directing a person's life. These forces will either lead you closer to God or further away from Him. It has to do with being drawn toward and through the narrow gate. Our divine destiny awaits each of us through that gate but we must allow ourselves to be led. The wide gate is the path we walk when seeking only what the world has to offer while neglecting our spiritual being.

Part of what makes surrender, surrender is the loss of self-assuredness. That prideful stubbornness of believing you know what's best for yourself. When you come to the point of realizing that all you have done has little meaning, or that all you've accomplished is to make a mess out of your life and the lives of those you love, you'll question your reason for being. You'll wonder why you were born, or if life is even worth living. You'll get to the point of knowing that you can't do it on your own, but wondering if God is really there to help you. As strange as it may seem this is a special time. This is what God has been waiting for. In other words, He has your attention. Now the coincidences can begin, especially, if you reach into the depths of your heart and ask Him into your life.

Part of the frustrations that I suffered in my old life was that I wanted to be a writer. I dreamt of writing professionally. Of course, I had no idea what it took to actually write well enough to be considered as such. For some reason, I left my English and grammar skills hovering around the ninth grade level. I think I was too busy excelling in Phys. Ed., lunch, and talking to the girls in study hall.

What I never considered in study hall was how frustrating it would be to discover a passion later in life, but not have the skills to pursue it.

While it may seen coincidental or an "accident", I believe there comes a time in every person's life when they are faced with the decision that ultimately determines whether they choose to move toward God or away from Him. Faced with losing everything, mine came on my knees in a little cabin up north. So much happened during that time that years later I still don't understand it all. But I do know that my surrendering to God changed the course of my life. It also let me see people and events in a whole other light.

Mandi, I'm not going to go into detail to disparage your mother because I was wrong in my actions. I hurt her so deeply that it created a hole in her soul that satan took advantage of. I'm convinced that's what an offense does to a person. When someone has been hurt or abused, evil can walk right in through that portal of anger, resentment, bitterness, vengeance, or retribution. This is why forgiveness is so incredibly important; it is the only way to close that open pathway to the dark spiritual world.

In your mother's state of anger and retribution, she seized the opportunity that my actions created. Using her own words, her only goal became: I am going to take it all. So after two years of marriage, your mother stripped me of twenty-five years of hard honest work.

At first, I resented her for that. Now, I see the spiritual world at work. I was not capable of making the changes needed in my life on my own. While I lived a meaningless existence I tried to fill the emptiness that I felt with material acquisition, conjured self-importance, and the collection of physical experiences that only resulted in my destiny growing more and more impatient. As long as I remained caught up in trying to satisfy the insatiable appetite for worldly things, I would never find the spirituality that I longed for, nor would I ever realize my passion to write. The problem was that my ego controlled my view of the world, and the last thing it wanted me to recognize was that the life it created was ineffective, selfish, and sinful.

Egos are funny that way. The very last thing they ever want is for the light of truthful self-examination to be turned on. Each of our egos' will have us believe that the entire world is wrong before ever looking into the mirror of responsibility.

Christ, in His classic, ageless wisdom, simple said, "Why do you look at the speck of dust in your brother's eye and pay no attention to the plank in your own eye."

Up in that little northern cabin, with my soul burning in the flame of God's discipline for hurting the people that I loved, my ego could no longer live with the pain it created. It lost its grip on my perception and it died, and it took the man I was and the life I knew with it.

I'm sure that your mother, whose ego remained squarely in vengeful control all that time, felt that she was justified in executing her plan for opportunistic acquisition, but I now see your mother, and even the evil that walked in through her pain, as a tool in God's hands. If your mother had given family counseling a chance, my ego would have remained intact and continued in its illusion that I was in control. The result of that would have been my remaining in the life that was destroying me. At forty-four, I was overweight, I had a mortgage that could finance a battleship, I was drinking enough alcohol to float it, and the stresses of my job were becoming so unbearable that I was on the "A" list for a heart attack. Which if it killed me would have fit nicely into satan's plan. That is really his only goal, for us to die in our sin. I think that is his way of paying God back for banishing him from heaven.

In that little cabin up north, I saw through the illusion I lived in and gave control of my life to God. Simply put, I gave up, not on life, mind you. I gave up trying to control it. My life had become unmanageable, and I had no one to blame but myself.

While my surrender did not extinguish the inferno in my soul, as there was more to learn from the pain. I knew, I mean I absolutely knew, that God's hand was firmly in control. And that from that moment forward He would take care of me. That didn't mean that everything was going to be hunky-dory. In fact, the worst was yet to come as your mother opened the floodgates of revenge and lies. And while your mother, in her wounded state, meant to do me harm, God meant it for good. Like Joseph, I lost everything and ended up exiled from those I loved.

The odd part is that she probably felt God answered her prayers. Her ego created the belief that she won out of righteous vengeance. Unfortunately, in reality, her illusions were maintained by greed, bitterness, and lies, and no one will ever find God there. On the other hand, I now see the devastation that befell me as necessary to truly wake me up. God was disciplining me. He would no longer tolerate my arrogance and sin.

Mandi, I still pray for your mother to this day. And I have begged her to forgive me, but she won't. And like so many other things forgiveness is a choice. To forgive me means that she will have to turn on the light of truth and understanding and acknowledge her own responsibilities. She will have to look at her own flaws and iniquities, and these are things that she does not want to see. Unfortunately, the alternative is: *What gaineth a man to gain the whole world, but lose his soul.*

In the early stages of my surrender, when I felt so lost, the coincidences began. I wish I'd taken notes as they piled up but I didn't. All I know is that one coincidence occurred after another. Soon they became a mountain of events that became impossible to ignore. I was being guided. Circumstances and events were leading me, and for the first time in my life my ego was not there to distort my perception. My life had direction from something greater than myself.

At one point, I found myself in a church service, and even though a couple of hundred people sat around me, I felt the sermon was for me and me alone. It seemed that God spoke directly to me through the man in the pulpit. He closed his message by saying, "God will forgive you, but you still have to pay the earthly consequences."

I knew what I had to do. I had to take responsibility for my actions and accept the consequences; consequences that would take five years to repay.

Next came the incredible coincidence of meeting a man who had Masters degrees in English composition and literature. He began to tutor me and critique my writing. Had I not met him I doubt I would have ever gained the skills needed to follow my dream. For the next two-and-a-half-years, he taught me.

Without my six-figure income my life style changed dramatically. I no longer had the means to support my self-abusive habits and indulgences, nor did I want to, God now filled the void in my life. I found employment of a physically nature, and I began caring for my health. I lost about sixty pounds, and the last time I checked, my blood pressure dropped from 146 over 96 to 116 over 72. The nurse told me: "You'll never have a heart attack with those numbers."

Currently my days are filled with physical activity, reading, writing, spiritual pursuits and the realization of my dreams. As hard as it may be to understand, the searing pain that once burned within me like a shovel full of coals has changed to a light that comforts and guides me. I will never go back to the rat-race, Mandi. The office politics, the miles long, red-tail-light-serpent of traffic jams, never ending bills, and living for tomorrow believing the ego's illusion that it will be better, is not for me. I've learned to live in the precious moment of now. I've tapped into the creative source of the great I Am. And even though I must constantly remind myself to keep my re-emerging ego in submission to my spirit, I am at peace. Today my most pressing goal is to let His wisdom guide me, often through coincidence, along the destiny of His choosing.

Prince Maxwell

Man's best friend. Max was every bit of that and even though he tried desperately to disguise it, he was so much more.

I remember how he slept at the bottom of the stairs, placing himself between any danger that might come into the house and our sleeping family. That was the theory anyway. When I walked down stairs at some early hour I'd have to step over Max stretched out practically snoring. I could only hope that his hyper-sensitive senses remained active as he slept, oblivious to his surroundings. I knew his hearing worked, because no matter how quiet I opened the refrigerator, or made the least little crinkling noise with a plastic wrapper, he became instantly alert assessing the situation.

Max, by instinct was a retriever. Not well developed, mind you, but a retriever nonetheless. When I threw a stick into the fire pit to be burned, Max felt compelled to bring it back to me. Yet, when I threw a ball and told him to fetch, he'd cock his head to one side with a look of blank anticipation as he waited for comprehension to burn through the perpetual fog he lived in. I didn't think he'd win the dumbest dog in the world contest, but I knew he'd get invited to the party.

Max did have occasions to show his true measure. One time a large Rottwieler came prowling around and threatening your mother. As he began to run toward her with his teeth barred and hair standing on end, Max came hurtling around the corner of the house. Fearlessly ferocious, he leapt into the middle of that huge snarling menace of a dog. The Rottwieler never knew what hit him. He left, yelping for mercy with his tail between his legs and Max in hot pursuit. We never saw that dog again.

That night, Max slept the sleep of the victorious, knowing that he did his job and protected his family. Max was entitled to his deep sleep of the weary warrior, but I found it difficult to tell the difference from when he just took a nap.

Max did exhibit a highly developed sense of humor. One time when he walked into the house, your mother saw that he carried something in his mouth. She held out her hand, and Max, always looking for ways to express himself, dropped a four inch crusty old dog turd in her hand. I guess your mother didn't really appreciate Max's little joke, but I think Max might have gotten a few "punch" lines in return.

I remember telling you guys, "Don't let him lick you on the face, he's a dog."

Then all of you would tell me things like: Oh, but Max loves us, or Max wouldn't do anything nasty, would ya Max?

I got a kick out of watching the blood drain from all of your faces as your mother told the story of Max's little joke.

I could have left it alone at that point and not said anything else. A considerate person would have. But as object lessons are so valuable, I couldn't really pass up such an opportunity and decided to ask, "Does anyone want a lick from Max?"

From the look on your faces I either unveiled some ghastly secret, or Max farted. Which, by the way, could not only bring a tear to your eye, it could also clear a room faster than anything I'd ever seen. Bottle a Max fart and the pepper spray people would be out of business.

Okay, I felt a little bad about Prince Maxwell no longer being considered in line for the throne, but at least you guys didn't let him lick your faces anymore.

Pets

Writing the last story about Max brought a flood of pet memories. I remember the time I went to my grandmother's whose Beagle had given birth to a litter of seven or eight puppies. I was three years old and those squirming bundles of joy would swarm all over me, licking and nipping at my ears making me laugh and fidget trying to keep them from sending me into hysterics.

Soon after, I graduated into pets I could capture. Of course, my Dad had a lot to do with that. One of our favorite things to do was to take our dog Pepper for runs in vacant fields. While Pepper frolicked in the open spaces, Dad and I hunted for exotic bugs and snakes.

To my mother's dismay, and my grandmother's horror, we used to find quite a few, which we always brought home in some old rusty can we found lying around. Since we were living with my grandmother at the time, the inevitable was bound to happen. One of my recently acquired foot-and-a-half long "pets" decided that he wouldn't mind moving into Grandma's house. Apparently, the can I left him in was less than suitable accommodations, because when I looked inside, he was gone.

Due to Grandma's phobia about snakes, I knew this minor infraction of loosing a "pet" in the house was punishable by keel-hauling, hung by the thumbs, the Pit and the Pendulum, or all of the above. In my preadolescent wisdom, it seemed that not saying anything was the only rational thing to do. My reasoning being that if I told Grandma we had an unexpected visitor, either of two terrible things was likely to occur. One was the shock of thinking about a snake loose in her house, slithering between her sheets some night might incapacitate her right there on the spot, or the overexertion of her chasing me through the house while beating me to a pulp might also cause her serious health problems. So, in the interest of Grandma's well-being, all I could do was wait and hope that the snake was smart enough to make his presence known to someone like me or my dad. Even through my young, eight year old perspective, I could see nothing good from the snake deciding that he wanted to introduce himself to Grandma. Between the snake, Grandma, or myself, I knew one of us would end up dead.

As luck would have it, a couple of weeks later, my mother watered the plants and there wrapped around the bottom of a clay pot catching a few rays was the endangered creature. To her credit Mom caught the rascal and let it go with me receiving the lecture of the century on what might have happened if my grandmother had found my little pet.

By the time I turned ten, I was into pets on a commercial scale in the form of raising hamsters. In a matter of a couple of years, I accumulated   a fairly respectable herd. In other words, we had hamsters coming out of our ears. I had hamster in cages in the garage, in cages in the house, and more times than not I had hamsters that consider the basement as open range. I don't remember ever making any money from raising hamster, but I do remember giving the family the worst case of fleas the doctor ever saw.

Next, I took a break from pets for a while as girls became more interesting, not to mention that most girls were not that crazy about snake hunting, turtle catching, or playing with baby alligators. I suppose the time I tried to impress my new girl friend by hand feeding my little gator only to have him sink his razor sharp teeth into my finger didn't help.

Then, I had pets mostly because the kids wanted them. Coerced into buying a small parrot named Chico, I remember how he ran up your mother's arm, across her shoulder, and bit her on the lip. I knew he was getting off to a bad start, first impression being what they are. How was I supposed to know that this type of parrot usually bonded with only one person in the family, in this case me. It turned out that Chico bit everybody. He bit your guys. He bit our friends.

He bit anybody foolish enough to get close to him who stuck out their finger and said, "Here Chico."

Occasionally, I let Chico out of his cage to fly around the room for a little exercise. When all of a sudden, one of the kids opened the front door, and poof, no more Chico. I followed him out of the house into the twilight of a late March afternoon, and watched as he flew up and came to rest in the neighbor's tree across the street. Neighbors whom I had not yet met as we'd just moved into the neighborhood.

Standing in the middle of the street, I could see Chico in his yellow and green plumage way up in the top of the tree. So there I stood in the middle of the street waving my arms over my head and hollering, "Here Chico, Chico come here."

After about fifteen minutes of me doing what looked like a ceremonial dance to the clouds, our neighbor Gretta, came out and said," I hope you don't mind me asking, but what exactly are you doing."

I pointed out Chico at the top of her tree and explained how he got loose.

Gretta looked at me satisfied that I was not a threat to the community and went back into her house. I continued to stand in the middle of the street waving my arms at the sky and calling out, "Here Chico!" all the while knowing that he'd never return.

As the sky darkened, I told myself that maybe it was for the best, since all he did was bite everybody anyway. Then, with one last wave, I wished him well in his new life, and told him to watch out for hawks.

About a week later a little girl knocked on our door, and when your mother answered, the little girl opened her cupped hands, exposing three green feathers. Then, she asked, "Is this your bird?"

Your mother, who wasn't able to positively ID Chico based on a few feathers, began thinking that he had been reduced to a flattened spot on the road, or some cat's dinner. She examined one of the feathers and said, "Yes, it could be."

The little girl replied, "When I was sitting in my room eating French fries, he flew in my window and took one."

Your mother asked, "Where is he now?"

The little girl responded, "He's still at my house eating French fires."

Since your mother didn't miss the biting little bastard, as she called him, she asked, "Would you like to keep him?"

The girl looked down at her fingers that had at least one bandage on each, and answered, "No, I don't think so. He bites."

Of course, I can't end a story about pets and mot mention Lord Maxwell. At one point, I thought I correctly characterized him as Max the Dummy, but lately I've been considering Max's historical position, and have come to the conclusion that his political campaign to become King worked after all.

Max only had two concerns throughout his strict daily regimen of napping in between strolls around the yard. Those two main concerns were, when was he going to be fed next, and the second being, how much.

As I trundled off to work one day, worrying about what bills had to wait until next payday, I envied Max wagging his tail without a concern in the world. At least he'd keep a watchful eye on things, especially those menacing squirrel brothers who tried to use the tree in our yard.

Who else but Max could lie around the house wherever he pleased, usually where someone would trip over him. Or how about how he'd stand at the door waiting for one of his naves to jump up and let him out. He got far more cuddling and attention than anyone else in the family. And compared to the rest of us, he lived a carefree, opulent lifestyle of leisure.

Come to think of it, I think the title of King Maxwell may have been appropriate after all.

Destiny

What other creatures have ever displayed a sense of destiny? Living or extinct, man is the only one I am aware of. And it doesn't seem to be a matter of brain size or function because elephants, whales, and dolphins all possess brains as large or larger than man's. They are capable of expressing a range of complex emotions and feelings, and they have language with communications skills that in many ways surpass our own. Whales can identify one another and communicate across vast expanse of ocean. Elephants emit sub-audible rumblings that can be sensed by other elephants for miles. Yet, with all their intelligence and emotions no other creature has ever erected even the simplest of shrines, or displayed a basic ritual for the purpose of worship or inspiration. Humankind is clearly set apart in regards to abstractions such as forgiveness, divinity, or destiny.

Even from the earliest traces of mankind, evidence has been uncovered of a universal curiosity for the spiritual realm.

Consider the implications of such curiosity. It doesn't matter what race, continent of origin, or time of existence, mankind has been instilled with a deep sense of spiritual inquisitiveness. How can that be explained from a purely evolutionary or psychological point of view? If all the other creatures that have lived never developed a spiritual sense, what made us different? Why, or how, did we cross the line?

I used to wonder about these things until I read in Genesis 1:27: *So God created man in His own image, in His image of God He created him; male and female He created them.* And in Genesis 2:7: *The Lord God formed man from the dust of the ground and breathed into his nostrils the breath of life, and man became a living being.*

F. Edward Marx   To Mandi, with Love

The apostle Paul tells us in Ephesians 1:11: *In Him we were all chosen, having been predestined according to the plan of Him who works out everything in conformity with the purpose of His will.*

In my arrogance and selfishness, I resisted God's plan for my life for forty-four years. I ignored my spiritual half and cavorted through life with the world as my playground. I allowed myself to distort the human gifts God gave me, such as good health, a bright mind, and a convincing manner into selfish manipulations designed to satisfy my worldly appetite. Then when I began to feel there wasn't any situation I couldn't control or anyone I couldn't manipulate, my pride became a form of self-worship. In essence, I believed, what need of God have I. And that was not my destiny.

Ephesians 1:4-6 tells us: *For He chose us in Him before the creation of the world to be holy and blameless in His sight. In love He predestined us to be adopted as His sons (and daughters) through Jesus Christ, in accordance with His pleasure and will....*

In retrospect, it now seems that my life had to unfold in such a manner in order to fully develop the gifts He gave me, yet make me humble enough to accept His direction. The really odd part is that I had to lose all the things of the world in order to find my peace. I now realize how little value I gained in the worldly things I consumed so voraciously. Other than the people that I loved, I miss very little of what I had and have found that living life at the surface of personality, in other words worried about what everyone else thinks, is really just living life in need, an existence defined by what one acquires. There was no spiritual destiny in how many cars I had or the size of my home. My true destiny could only be found in what laid underneath my ego. It's not easy, and not everyone rises to the challenge, but for those who do, finding one's destiny is finding God's purpose in their life.

The search begins with pride. That must be stripped away first. Pride is the veil that keeps each of us from seeing the spiritual reality of who we truly are. Humility is the key that will unlock the door to the plan God has waiting for us.

Beneath fear is love. So much love is lost because people are afraid to face their fears. They won't take off the mask of the ego for fear of being hurt, ridiculed, or failing.

Beneath hate is courage. It is so easy to hate. Real courage is to peer into one's self, looking past the pain, through the injury to the heart and mind in order to close the wound to the soul.

Opposite of greed is connectivity to the human race. Service to others is the food of the soul. When you really want to find meaning in your life, give something of yourself. In that moment of helping someone in need you will feel more satisfied, more alive, than any other time.

The list goes on: under bitterness is forgiveness, under jealousy is confidence, and under ego is a person's true spiritual self.

That is destiny. Open yourself to finding your true spiritual side, and you will find what God has planned for you.

Typhoon Pamela

The first time I heard about Typhoon Pamela, she was just a young blustery storm twirling about in the western Pacific Ocean. As she approached the Philippine Island of Luzon where I was stationed, the Naval Air Base Commander declared storm condition Alpha. We prepared the base and the squadron's aircraft for a major downpour, but nothing too serious. Storm condition Alpha lasted for a couple of days with everyone hoping she would veer off, and we would only get the rain. Pamela, however had other plans.

Gathering strength and moisture, she plotted directly toward us. Storm condition Bravo was announced. Consequently, all the planes that could fly took off for some safe section of the world, leaving behind a skeleton ground crew, which of course, included me.

Since it was my buddies and my job to take care of the airplanes, no airplanes meant, no jobs, so we were placed on duty relief status and were free to go to our houses in town and ride out the storm.

Strom condition Charlie, the most severe classification the Navy issues, became imminent, and once declared the gates to the base would be closed. I had to decide whether to stay on or off base for the duration for the storm. Infused with the spirit of adventure, and convinced of my immortality, I wanted to be off base hanging out with my buddies and friends.

Young and foolish, we were oblivious to the danger of riding out a typhoon in structures built of plywood and corrugated tin.

Of course, one does not just go home and wait for a typhoon. Certain preparations must be made. The first was to go to the base liquor store and buy all the booze my ration card allowed. Then, I went to the grocery store and bought all the food and candles I could carry. After that, I went to the Sari-Sari store, the Philippine version of a party store, and purchased a wagonload of San Miguel beer. Finally, with enough food and booze to supply the New Years Eve celebration in Times Square, I felt ready for the typhoon.

By this time it had been pouring a river from the sky for several days; electricity, ice, and fresh water were only memories. There was, however, so shortage of running water. The streets flowed with swift knee-high streams. No one could tell were the real river ended and the town began, and neither could the fish. When I waded outside, I found it important to watch out for snakes and rats that swam along looking for something or someone to climb onto.

As Pamela neared, the rain began to come down sideways in a proverbial wall of water. It soaked through windows and walls, with every pan, bucket, pail and jar positioned under a leak in the roof. The larger containers were strategically located so that they collected water from two or more leaks at the same time. The ground floor of my two-story house was under a foot of water, and all of us camped out on the second floor with nothing else to do but empty catch pails, eat, drink, and be merry. We had no choice. Pamela was in charge of all our lives for the foreseeable future.

It had been raining sideways for two days when I began thinking that things couldn't get much worse, and wondering how long it might take to build an ark. Even though the effects of being cooped up in a couple of small rooms didn't bother me, it seemed to be have taken a toll on my friends, who at that point were engaged in a farting contest. An event that required the contestant to bend over with a lit match next to his exposed rear end as he tried to conjure some flatulence. The winner, as judge by his peers, was the one who shot out the most spectacular flame.

After the forth full day of the typhoon party, the fun was pretty much over. Supplies ran low, and the boredom factor had risen right off the scale. The high point at this time consisted of my snail winning the snail races. A race that began by picking the biggest snails off the wall and placing them in the center of a rope ring and waiting to see whose snail got to the edge first.

F. Edward Marx   To Mandi, with Love

When I thought that things couldn't get any worse, Typhoon Pamela actually arrived.

The boredom that plagued us ended. It had been replaced by sheer amazement and occasional fits of terror induced by Mother Nature's awesome power. Cars slid down the street sideways and piled up at one end. Sheets of corrugated tin, previously someone's roof, twisted through the air like a giant buss-saw. Uprooted trees sailed overhead as if by magic, and the worst of all possible occurrences—we ran out of beer.

We had done pretty well up to that point, but when Steve drained the last beer and crushed the can against his forehead, I knew we were in serious trouble. Someone would have to go to the Sari-Sari store, normally a trip of about a hundred-and-fifty-yards; however, under Pamela's conditions, Moby Dick had a better chance of actually arriving.

Since nobody volunteered for this hazardous mission, and we wanted to be fair about who would risk their life for a case of beer, we decided to draw straws, toothpicks actually. Right away, I knew I was in trouble. If we were drawing for a trip to Tahiti, I wouldn't stand a chance; but make the contest for an opportunity to drown in a raging typhoon, and the odds skyrocketed in my favor. With only two toothpicks left, it was my turn to draw. Tim bravely held them out. I could see the concern chiseled into his face as he wondered who would get the short one. He needn't have worried, and just for the formality, I grabbed a toothpick.

Everyone cheered and congratulated me, and said, "Hurry back."

Since I had never actually been in a typhoon before, let alone go for a stroll, I wasn't exactly sure what to wear. Boots wouldn't help as the water flowing downstairs in my living was above the tops of any I possessed. An umbrella was useless—typhoons eat them for breakfast. As it was pointless to try to stay dry, I settled on the typhoon fashion of flipflops, shorts, and no shirt. Instead, I wore a big black plastic bag with holes cut out for my head and arms. To finish my ensemble, I fasten the garbage bag around my waist with a rope accessory.

Off I went on my quest for beer.

One step out of the door and the rain slapped me in the face while the wind knocked me down into the river flowing out of my house. Realizing this was not going to be a scene from **Singing In the Rain**, I leaned into the wind as it lifted me off the ground and blew away one of my flipflops. The only way I made forward progress was to not let go of my current handhold until I had something else to grab onto.

Should anyone else ever plan to go for a walk in a typhoon, there is one more thing I suggest watching out for. That is flying lizards. It's obvious that a typhoon is not very particular as to what it picks up to throw at you, with wet slimy leaves one of its favorites; however, a small green and yellow lizard that is trying to cling to your nose and mouth is just enough of a distraction so that pieces of the neighbor's house become a real problem. And there is no telling what else might be blowing in the wind.

The rain stung my face with a thousand wet needles a second. The current tried to take my feet one way while the wind blasted my body another. The walk that usually took me less than a minute to complete began to have a feeling of eternity to it. Then, all of a sudden when I looked up during a lull between sheets of gust driven rain, the door to the Sari-Sari store stood right in front of me.

The live-in owners were glad to see me as they hadn't had much business in the last couple of days. We talked about the weather, and I partied with them for a couple of hours hoping that the wind might die down. Eventually, feeling guilty over my friends who were out of beer I decided to be on my way. I tied my purchases into the garbage bag that I'd worn for the trip to the store, grabbed my case of beer, and headed back into the deluge. Two steps later the wind knock me down and I found myself in a wrestling match with sumo Pamela for who was going to end up with possession of my beer and food. Eventually, she tired of my tenacity and I was able to crawl along with one hand grabbing whatever I could reach, while my other hand pushed my cherished groceries forward. The trick turned out to be to push my stuff forward then lie on it while I reached for a new handhold.

Once back at the house, I gave Steve his crushed waterlogged cigarettes. Stan received his bag of potato chip soup, and Tim just shook his head and asked, "What, no pretzels?"

The Maid

My reminiscing about Typhoon Pamela triggered a host of other fond memories. In my illustrious eight-year naval career in which I never served on board ship one day, I had the opportunity to travel all around the Western Pacific. As luck would have it, I drew an assignment to an anti-submarine warfare squadron at Barbers Point, Hawaii. Which is located right across the bay from Pearl Harbor. Every eighteen-months my land based squadron and I deployed to places like Guam, Japan, Okinawa and my favorite the Philippines.

In 1976 the Philippines was a young man's Disneyland. As a third world economy even my pittance of an enlisted man's salary was a king's ransom. The rate of exchange was seven-and-a-half Philippine pesos to one American dollar. A cold bottle of San Miguel beer, drank in the bar, listening to live rock and roll, cost two pesos, or about twenty-eight measly cents. And if I went to the Sari-sari store I could get a one-liter bottle of Pepsi or a beer for one peso, or fourteen cents.

On my meager salary, I bought an old Chevy station wagon, rented an apartment in town, and secured the services of what every twenty-four-year-old needs, a maid.

Leeta was a stitch, constantly making me laugh. She recently moved to the "big" city after having lived all her life in a small village carved out of the jungle. Things like a toaster, iron, or electric frying pan were wonders to her. She couldn't grasp how they got warm without a fire underneath them. Since she couldn't speak any English and I couldn't speak her native dialect of Tagalag, explanations were never easy. All of our communication consisted of an impromptu, made up version of sign language. I'd conjure up some exaggerated motions that I thought conveyed my desires or intentions, and she would start doing what she thought I wanted. Then we would make adjustments accordingly. With the usual adjustment of me giving up and letting her do whatever she was doing in the first place.

A typical conversation went something like this. I motioned for her to follow me outside to help wash the car. Standing in front of the car, I acted out my need for a bucket by imitating her washing clothes. Then, as I pointed at the car with the water hose, I motioned like I'm washing it. It would have been easier to get the bucket myself; however, as cleaning supplies were her strict domain, I didn't know where she kept the pails. After completing my interpretive dance titled: The Wash of the Dirty Car, I saw the glimmer of comprehension in her eyes.

She went off to get me a pail, but when I looked up a few moments later from where I cleaned inside the car, I noticed her filling up the large washtub with water from the hose. Since I didn't want to use the whole bottle of soap on one wash, I tried to try to tell her that I wanted the smaller bucket. At this point it's important to keep in mind that the Tagalag word for water is tubig, (pronounced too big) and the word for what or why is baquet, (pronounced ba-ket). As I walked over to her waving my hands around and saying the bucket is too big, she looked at me as if horns were growing out of my head. With a look of exasperation she continued filling the washtub with water (tubig) while nodding and saying, "Yes, yes, tubig." Then she'd shake the running hose as if adding emphasis and repeating, "Tubig, tubig."

Caught up in the moment, I excitedly told her, "No, no, the bucket is too big, get a smaller bucket."

Puzzled by my strange behavior, she questioned, "Baquet?"

At this point I realized the futility of it all and just started washing the car from the bucket that was big enough to wash all the cars in Philadelphia.

Leeta also had some very strange notions regarding health care. One time she pointed to the swelling in her cheek and rattled the car keys at me. That being the well understood sign for me to drive her somewhere. Thinking that I would be taking her to the dentist, we drove through the back streets of Olongapo. We wound our way

F. Edward Marx   To Mandi, with Love

through smelly alleys only inches wider than the car, and suffocated in a traffic jam caused by a stubborn water buffalo. Finally, she signaled me to pull over next to a crinkled old woman sitting in a rickety makeshift concession stand. Upon closer inspection, I realized this was not your typical pharmacy. Her shelves were stocked full of batwings, frog heads, insects, herbs, snake gallbladders, sticks, leaves and a thousand things that I didn't recognize but was afraid to ask. The two of them conversed for a few minutes when the old woman began nodding her head and digging around in a darkened corner. Finally, she turned as if she carried some precious artifact and handed Leeta a twig. Paying for the stick, Leeta bowed slightly in reverence to the old sage, and home we went.

On the way back I thought, *she must be going to make an herbal tea from the stick or maybe she is going to suck on it to extract whatever medicinal qualities it might have.* I dropped her off satisfied that she was all set with some remedy unknown to western medicine. I must admit my surprised when I returned to see her with a towel wrapped around her head and the medicine twig poking out between the towel and the outside of her cheek.

One time, I had a bad stomachache. Considering the abuse I put my digestive system through that was never really any surprise. In her sweet compulsion to help me, Leeta always offered her most well intended care. But it never really worked out that way. This time she laid me down on the Papa-san sofa and signaled me to wait for her return. A few moments later she sat down next to me with a lit candle and a tall empty glass. As I tried to inquire or protest, she engaged me in this long tirade of intense dialogue, of which I understood, nothing. Knowing that I never won these one-way arguments, I let her proceed. She lifted my shirt, dripped hot wax into my navel, and stuck the candle into the hot wax. Next, she covered my flaming bellybutton with the glass. As the flame flickered out due to lack of oxygen, she lifted up the glass showing me that it stuck to me due to the partial vacuum. Excitedly, she tried to explain that the magic of vacuum was sucking out the pain.

On the other hand Leeta was terrified of doctors. When she stepped on a rusty nail I took her to the clinic to get a tetanus shot. If I hadn't known better, I'd have thought by the look of terror on her face that I was taking her to appear before the Spanish Inquisition. Nevertheless, that treatment was apparently not sufficient. After her injection, she made me wait in line with her while a street-vendor, witch doctor, milked a Philippine cobra for its venom. Then, he mixed it with some white chalky substance and sold it to the people in line who drank it for five pesos a thimble glass full. Apparently, she was more concerned about tetanus than I first thought.

My six-month deployment went by all too quickly, and as military people have been doing for thousands of years, it came time to say good-bye. We parted the best we could, trying to keep the tears to a minimum, but I knew I would never forget her innocent charm and her lovely face. I have regretted leaving her more that once.

Tolerance

It saddens me to the core of my heart and soul when I watch the news or read about people who inflict pain, humiliation, terror and even death upon another human being, and all in the name of differences, be they cultural, ethnic or sexual.

I'm disgusted when I witness some act of prejudice and hatred based solely on a person's genetic heritage. Something none of us has the slightest control over. Then, when I see that evil being taught to a child I'm almost nauseated. Here's a child who knows no reason for any animosity or fear of someone because they are different, yet some ignorant adult is willing to lay the double tragedy of prejudice on to him of her. The reason I say double tragedy is because hate poisons not only those it's poured upon but the container that holds it as well.

People are different for a reason. Through the science of biology along with the study of the climatic influence on favorable genetic adaptations, we can easily see how the human race has adapted to differences in their surrounding environments. Just by looking at people who have lived and adapted to extreme environments such as the Arctic, we see a race of people who are short, compact, and sturdy. This allows for less body area to be exposed to the elements, and a stature designed for conserving heat. Travel to the opposite of heat extremes and you will find a race of people who are very tall, with dark skin. Skin that is tolerant of intense sunlight with their bodies structured to reduce and easily eliminate body heat; facilitated by long thin extremities that expose more body surface to the ambient air. While I realize that I am oversimplifying a very complex biological process. The fact is we are all the result of our genetic ancestry; no more or no less endowed than anyone else.

One of the many lessons that I have learned in my travels is that people of all races and walks of life want and need basically the same things. No matter where I traveled, whole populations of people were just striving to raise their families, looking for opportunities, and wanting to live in an environment with enough personal freedom to pursue their goals and aspirations.

One time, I was part of an installation team helping to install some complex computer equipment. As part of the installation, I helped train the production staff in the operation of our systems. Everyone learned the operation with the exception of a man of a different race. He was having a difficult time catching on to the proper sequence of commands and prompts. A short time later, I realized that this man couldn't read. At first, I was irritated that this company's hiring policy would allow for illiteracy. Then after a few moments, I thought, *you pompous ass*. Here is a man that has not had a fraction of the opportunities that life has offered you. How can you stand in judgment and criticize his life of which you know nothing about.

I took him aside and together we drew the icon symbols in the proper sequence of operation. He practiced following the symbols, and after a short time he was operating the system properly. Not only did he become one of the most conscientious operators in that facility, but the look of gratitude he offered filled me with one of the deepest and warmest sense of accomplishment that I have ever felt. In the flash of his expression, he communicated his sense of relief in keeping his job, feeding his family, and progressing with his skills.

Hatred and prejudice only breed pain and suffering, they solve nothing. They only serve the destroyer's purpose by becoming the fabric that he weaves to cover the hearts and minds of mankind.

For anyone who has no tolerance for others because they are different, he should ask himself: what is it about me that needs hate to hide behind? And if he can ever truthfully look into the mirror of self-examination, he will see someone enslaved by his own fears and delusions.

A Blanket and a Swan

Strolling along the edge of the lake one late December afternoon, Bobby and I watched as Max frolicked on the newly formed ice. Suddenly, an injured swan leapt out in front of us. Flapping furiously, it tried to fly away. As the swan beat its wings against the ice, I could see that half of its right wing was missing. Max took off in hot pursuit after the poor bird, but at my call, he returned and left the injured creature alone. We continued walking, but I couldn't stop thinking of the swan with no wing. Eventually, I realized it was doomed to a fate of either starvation or predation.

Further along, Bobby saw some friends, so he left me alone with Max and my thoughts. The image of the hapless swan isolated and alone sitting on the frozen lake haunted me. Walking along, I found myself in this knock down, drag out, wrestling match with my conscience. Torn between thoughts about the natural order of survival of the fittest versus feelings of compassion for injured wild life, I wondered what I could do. By the time I got home I had the bright idea of calling the Department of Natural Resources (DNR). They gave me the number of a woman in the area licensed to rescue injured wildlife.

I figured I was on a roll. One more simple phone call and my good deed would be complete.

I phoned the woman.

She confirmed that if it's not rescued, the swan would die. Then she asked, "When can you bring it to me?"

After a lengthy pause while I tried to figure out exactly where my plan went wrong, I asked, "Bring it out to you? I thought that was your job."

"No," she answered, "I have no way to get it right now, and it would really help me if you could catch it and bring it to me."

F. Edward Marx   To Mandi, with Love

"Bring it to you?"
"Yes, just throw a blanket over it and it should be fine."
"Should be fine?"
"Yes, he may spit and hiss but he probably won't bite."
"Won't bite?" I thought about the team of rescuers it would take to get me out of the lake should the ice not hold and reluctantly agreed.

Mentally preparing myself for my first swan rescue, I tucked one of Max's old blankets under my arm. As I walked back out to where I last saw the swan I couldn't help wondering about the probably won't bite part.

Half hoping that the swan had moved and I wouldn't find it, I flashed back to the time when I watched an adult swan protect it's young from the neighbor's Cocker Spaniel. He cracked the dog with his huge wings stunning it. The he grabbed the dog by the fur on its neck and proceeded to beat it unconscious with his wings. The Cocker Spaniel never knew what hit him, and if the owner's hadn't come to the dog's rescue the swan was in the process of dragging the dog into the lake to drown it. The idea of getting up close and personal to such ferocity was not something I looked forward too. Typically, as my luck goes, the swan was right where I left it—out in the middle of the new ice.

Not to be daunted by trivial matters such as thin ice, freezing to death, or losing a nose or an ear, I tried to slowly creep up on the bird. Who by this point was giving me its undivided attention. I got as close to the injured swan as its comfort zone allowed before it bolted across ice.

The swan took off flapping and running as fast as it could manage and the chase was on.

The new ice was especially slick. Only by using the small patches of snow for traction could I propel myself forward. Once off the snow I had to slide along carefully maintaining my balance as I aimed for another patch.

Across the lake we scrambled. The swan flapping and honking, and me running a couple of steps then sliding a few feet, running a step, sliding a foot. Slowly closing in on the scared bird, I got the blanket ready to throw hoping to end the dangerous race over unsure ice.

Of course, nothing is ever that simple. Just as I was about to toss the blanket, the wind whipped across the lake making it impossible to aim the billowing cloth. At this point, I began to imagine the neighbors as they watched me doing my Don Quixote impression of fighting a sail. I knew that anyone looking had to be thinking: *The lunatic is on the loose again.*

Once more I closed in on the swan. As I readied the blanket, I slipped and fell in a bone-crunching heap as the swan scrambled away honking madly. Each time I got close, I either slipped and fell or threw the blanket into the wind and missed. Occasionally, I displayed my creativity by falling down and throwing the blanket, all in the name of rescue and compassion.

Of course, the swan was not in complete agreement with my valiant attempt to save its life, so we proceeded like this across most of the lake. A poor injured creature honking and scrambling for its freedom and a wild blanket-billowing-man running, slipping and falling behind it. I'm not sure if the swan eventually tired, or if it just gave up in order to save it's dignity, but I finally got close enough to throw the blanket and capture the poor beast.

Keeping it tightly wrapped with only its head sticking out, I carried the hissing and spitting creature home.

Tracking Bobby down, I enlisted his help to take the swan to the wildlife rescuer.

Bobby climbed onto the back seat and I handed him the wrapped, hissing and snarling bird. The only instruction I could think of was, don't let him get loose while I'm driving.

Although he was not overly thrilled about his duties of wild swan guard, eight-year-old Bobby kept the bird subdued for the trip. I could tell by the hisses and spits followed by the screams of, "He's moving," that an eight year old boy and a yearling swan were pretty evenly matched.

By the time we arrived, Bobby was in tears. The swan was wrapped so tight that it could hardly breath, and from what I could tell they were both relieved to part company.

The wildlife rescuer looked at the swan's wing and told us that it was an old injury. Probably a big turtle got it when it was a baby. Then she assured us that she would find it a suitable home.

Both Bobby and I knew that we had saved the swan's life. We left her farm that night feeling like the stars shined just a little brighter in our corner of the world.

The Polar and Bear Club

One pleasant February evening, if there is such a thing in Michigan, I decide to go for a walk with Max. We stopped to pick up his buddy, Bear the Boviae, as he too like our evening strolls across the lake. The three of us ventured toward some small islands that Max and Bear liked to explore. Since the swan episode, I had confidence in the ice as I unintentionally tested it from one end of the lake to the other.

Suddenly, which of course is the only way these things happen, I dropped through the ice up to my neck. Bear, who walked right next to me, also took the express elevator down to the aquatic floor. Needless to say, it didn't take me long to figure out this was not going to be that pleasant of a walk. I hollered at Max to stay back as it appeared he wanted to help. He was excitedly jumping up and down and running circles around the hole Bear and I struggled in. I sure didn't need another dog in the mix. It was painfully obvious to me that one animal and a waterlogged disaster was bad enough because at that moment Bear was trying to scramble out using my head and shoulders as his personal stepladder.

After untangling myself from the crazed swamp thing, I lifted myself onto the edge of the ice even though it felt like I weighed about a ton-and-a-half. Unfortunately, the ice was only rated at a one-ton capacity, so it broke again, plunging me face first back into the slush-and-panic-stricken-boviae-filled-hole. I tried lifting myself out a second and a third time only to break through the ice and splash back into the frigid water.

Tiring quickly, I needed to regain my composure. It was then that I noticed one of the small islands only about thirty yards away. Desperate to end my February swim, not to mention get away from a hysterical dog who was literally on my back, I began climbing onto the ice to break it intentionally. With each new break, I moved a couple of feet closer to the shore. Eventually, I ice-breakered myself into the shallow water of the island and casually stepped onto the beach. Unfortunately, Bear the ice dog, was still whining and swimming in the original hole. He was so panicked that he hadn't figure out that I had escaped. Yelling at him, I finally got his attention, and for the first time he noticed that I was no longer with him in the stunningly cold water. It was a good thing that he figured it out because I was rapidly losing interest in standing around drip-drying in fifteen-degree temperatures, and I certainly wasn't about to return to the realm of the bluegills to retrieve him.

We made a beeline for home.

By the time we got back, Bear looked like a snow cone with legs, and I the proverbial abominable snowman. My clothes had frozen solid except for my elbows and knees.

Everyone thought it quite funny as I walked into the house and climbed into a hot shower clothes and all. After several minutes of the life saving warmth, I took inventory of my anatomy and I realized that I'd be okay.

I never planned on becoming a member of the Polar Bear club, but taking a dip through February ice with a dog named Bear, should at least qualify me for honorable mention.

Projection

Projection is a slippery psychological concept to grasp. It is something that each of us does, yet few understand. It is part of the energy of thought that we push out into the world around us, but more importantly it is how that energy comes reflecting back through that person's perception.

Projection is responsible for the reality we create in each of our lives, and it is one of the principles of Karmic law.

Karma is best described as you reap what you sow. If you create a world in which you readily lie and try to deceive those around you, you will live in a world of suspicion and belief that everyone around you is not to be trusted.

Allow selfishness or greed into your life and it will end up tainting each relationship as you will believe that everyone wants something from you.

If you project a sense of helplessness, you will become a victim. Cause others pain and you will feed the psychological cancer that will destroy yourself.

On the other hand, if you project a sense of strength and confidence, you will find yourself empowered and accomplished.

Genuinely love and care for people, and you will be deeply endeared in the hearts of others.

Put forth the best that human nature has to offer and you will bring out the best in those around you.

Projection may be the single most important characteristic that we should understand, yet few make the effort. I've written this simple poem that may help just a little. After reading it ask your self: What will I find within?

F. Edward Marx   To Mandi, with Love

In a large oak tree that edged the woods the wise old owl perched.
A skunk came by and asked the owl, "What will I find within?"
The owl asked, "The woods you left what were the creatures like?"
"Dirty, smelly, and very bold," the skunk hastily replied.
The owl sighed and then explained, "These creatures are the same."

A fox came by and asked the owl, "What will I find within?"
The owl asked, "The woods you left what were the creatures like?"
"Most lied and cheated and snuck around," the fox slyly replied.
The owl sighed and then explained, "These creatures are the same."

 A doe came by and asked the owl, "What will I find within?"
The owl asked, "The woods you left what were the creatures like?"
"Most were quiet, gentle, and very kind," the deer cordially replied.
The owl smiled and then explained, "These creatures are the same."

The Dawning of Civilization

Most anthropologists agree that discovering the techniques for cultivation and agriculture were the basic skills needed for civilization to occur. Learning to grow crops provided mankind a stable enough food source to begin building more permanent structures along with meeting the needs of larger groups of people.

This line of thinking is all well and good; however, it does not adequately address why it took mankind several hundreds of thousands of years of hunting and gathering to finally realize that it would be a lot easier just to become farmers.

I would like to add my own as yet unproven theory to the real dawning of civilization. Remember Ew and Ah, the two young prehistoric guys, who like to roam. Well, a long cold winter had depleted the tribes' meager stores and forced our two intrepid wanders to leave the starving members of their camp in search of food. As they trudged away in hip-deep snow, they promised to find "something" and bring it back.

Ew and Ah had been traveling through a bleak, rugged, winter landscape for several days when all of a sudden the weather took a turn for the worse. Had they known about the impending storm they'd never have left the warmth of their home campfire. Unfortunately, prehistoric weatherman weren't any better at predicting the forecast than the weathermen of today, so the boys got caught in a cold, howling, winter blast.

Half frozen and craving shelter, they saw a small opening in the rocks that looked to be a cave. Shivering uncontrollably from the ice, and freezing snow, they figured just about any shelter would do. As they rushed into the cave, they suddenly realized they weren't the only occupants. While a gnarly, old, hibernating cave bear is known to have under developed social skills, our two prehistoric Popsicles weren't in any good mood either.

All hell broke loose as a fur-flying, teeth-breaking brawl took place for who was going to spend the night warm and cozy, or wet and cold. Eventually, the bear decided that if they wanted the cave that bad they could have it. So he packed his things and left, taking with him only a few small pieces of the boys.

Well, that little tussle warmed the guys enough that they were able to build a fire and begin making themselves at home.

Ew looked around satisfied with their new digs and said, "Nothing like a little exercise before dinner to make you hungry, what's to eat?"

Ah looked over at him dejectedly as he held up the stick he was sucking on and grunted, "Want some?"

"No that's okay," Ew answered, "I had one for lunch. Let's look around, it looks like someone lived here before the bear."

As Ew scrounged in a pile of rocks, he found some slimy, wet, fermented grain lying in a puddle of water. Excitedly, he yelled to Ah, "Hey look what I found!"

Even though, slimy grain mixed with fermented water may not seem that appetizing, to frozen, bone-starved cave men, it still wasn't any good.

They ate it anyway.

After his third mouthful Ah said, "This stuff taste awful."

Ew replied, "Yeah, it's terrible, but I'm so hungry I'm going to eat some more."

So they sat, soaking in the warmth of their fire eating stale grain and drinking the fermented brew.

Ah sighed and said, "I'm sure feeling better."

Ew swallowed another scoop of grain and juice, and with his mouth full, garbled, "Du know, dis stuff ain't so bad once du get dused to it."

Ah gulped down another handful and slurred, "Is's terrific, give me sssome more."

While they basked in the glow of their Spartan hearth, drinking the left over fermented water, Ah began retelling their bear story. "We sure showed that ol' beer a thing or two...didn't we?"

"Ha, Ha, Ha" Ew laughed. "You said, beer, instead of bear. Maybe that's what we should call this stuff--beer."

"That's great," Ah chortled. "But how do we get some more?"

They spent the rest of that night looking around for more beer. Unfortunately, all they found was a large stash of properly stored grain. Then, when they tried adding water nothing happened. They correctly guessed there was more to this beer thing than met the eye.

So what did discovering beer have to do with the dawn of civilization? Well, it seems that in our hero's quest to make more beer they needed a lot of grain to experiment with. Apparently, learning the fermentation process was fraught with problems. Especially like times when they thought that bear piss was the missing ingredient.

Since the tribe wouldn't let them have any of the small amount of grain that they could gather to feed themselves, the boys had to find a way to come up with a surplus of grain for their beer making experiments. Noticing that the grain the tribe gathered grew in the ground, the boys tried planting a few of their seed kernels. Of course, everybody laughed at first--wasting their food in the ground that way. But, everybody stopped laughing when little green sprouts appeared where the guys had planted their seeds. In order not to be out done by a couple of youngsters, the chief instructed everyone to plant and grow grain.

Needless to say, that fall the boys had all the grain they needed to finally be able to make more beer.

What If We Are The Only Ones

I recently read somewhere that over ninety-five percent of all the plant and animal species that ever lived on this planet are extinct.

While it is a commendable and worthwhile effort to protect and conserve endangered species, it is also inevitable that some will be lost.   Undeniably, for the four billion year history of this planet, extinction has been part of the natural order.

The age of the dinosaurs lasted approximately one-hundred-and-sixty-million years, a period in which they dominated life on earth. Their reign ended about sixty million years ago when what many believe was a catastrophic impact from an asteroid.

Geological evidence for this has been found in a thin but global wide layer of the element iridium that was deposited at the sixty million year striation in the fossil record. Under the iridium layer are dinosaur fossils. Above the layer they are absent. Iridium is rare on earth; however, meteors and asteroids are believed to contain it in relatively large amounts. The theory is that an asteroid containing iridium crashed into the earth. The resulting explosion ejected enough debris into the atmosphere to create a dust ring that encompassed the entire planet. This altered the climate on a global scale with both plants and animals unable to survive. The iridium seeded dust eventually settled back to earth, covering the surface and the skeletal remains of the dinosaurs.

Philosophically, we can speculate on what if that catastrophic event sixty million years ago never occurred. Would mammals have emerged to populate the earth? Would humankind have risen to the pinnacle of dominance, or might the dinosaurs have continued as the ruling species? Then, what of God's plan for creatures made in His image?   Creatures that might one day travel to the stars and seed planets with genetic experiments of their own?

How about the possibility of another asteroid hurtling through space with our name on it? Pictures of the moon show the cratered record of its bombardment. A history that earth has not escaped, it just has erosion, oceans, and volcanism to cover and heal the scars. There is a cataclysmic event in our future. The study of our past tells us that it is only a matter of time.

Were we given the means, the intellect, and the time to avoid extinction? Is it our destiny to populate the stars? Have we been given all that we need to insure that mankind will live on?

We are beginning the third millennium. That's two thousand years of western civilization and about ten thousand years since the earliest civilizations have been keeping records. We certainly have come a long way in the last ten thousand years. We have over populated the planet. We have polluted our atmosphere, our oceans, and our fresh water. We have depleted the great fisheries of the seas, and even as we continue to abuse our atmosphere we cut down and burn the rain forest that is the filter for that polluted air. And if all that's not enough to rid ourselves from this planet, we have developed magnificently effective ways to kill each other.

Yes, we have come a long way in the last ten thousand years, but I find myself wondering if we will make it through the next one hundred.

Each time I gaze out into the star filled, night sky, I feebly contemplate the magnitude of the universe and our destiny within it. Marveling at the sheer number of stars, I have come to understand that many of those pin points of light that look like a star are actually a distant galaxy unto itself. The vastness of our universe is more than any mind can comprehend, with no limit to the wonders, mysteries and discoveries out there awaiting us.

Unfortunately, there is a problem; an almost insurmountable barrier. It is distance itself. Our closets neighboring star is Alpha Centauri. And even though it is the star next door, it is four and a half light years away, or approximately twenty six trillion (26,000,000,000,000) miles.

The center of our Galaxy is thirty thousand (30,000) light years away from Earth, with our closest neighboring galaxy, called M31, two million (2,000,000) light years away. It's mind boggling to look up at a distant star or galaxy and realize that mankind did not even exist when that light in the night sky actually left its point of origin. It's also a little disconcerting when I pick out a star and realize it may no longer physically exist. That star could have gone nova fifty thousand 50,000 years ago, but because it's sixty thousand (60,000) light years away, we won't know of its fate for another ten thousand (10,000) years.

My amazement grows when I consider things like the earth is the exact distance from the sun for liquid water to be readily available. This is considered an essential ingredient for life.

Coincidentally, the moon is the exact distance from the earth to create seasonal stability as it provides a counter gravitational weight to reduce the earth's wobble. And astrophysicists tell us that without the orbiting giants, Jupiter and Saturn, life on earth would not exist at all. Apparently, their massive gravitational forces attract and collect most of the stellar debris that careens through our solar system keeping those flying mountains from crashing into us. Without Jupiter and Saturn as our cosmic protectors, Earth would never have been left unmolested long enough for life to exist and flourish.

I won't even try to explain ideas like the force of gravity being the exact quantum value that is required to create orbital systems. But without that exactness everything would either be sucked into everything else or everything would fly apart. All I know is, here we are, alive and thriving in factors of coincidence that are so astronomically rare that they may not exist anywhere else. And if they do exist anywhere else it is a **long** way away.

Will we ever fulfill our ultimate destiny of reaching the stars? Not as long as we continue to be caught up in intolerance, hate, ethnic differences and wars. Only if we unite in the goal of interstellar travel will we ever have a chance to experience the universe and to reach the potential that it means to be made in the image of God. No one race or country will ever have all the resources or talents needed to conquer the barrier of space. Only a united mankind has that potential.

Considering what profound fools we are, and the awesome consequences of freewill, just maybe the barrier of space was put there by design. Possibly, a bunch of selfish, egotistical idiots are not meant to trash the universe. Considering our poor track record as custodians of this bejeweled planet, we don't deserve to be out there.

I've heard and read about all kinds of alien abductions, unidentified flying objects and incredible events like Roswell, in which eyewitness accounts describe a crashed flying saucer, alien beings, and a government cover up. But, if you consider a civilization capable of interstellar or inter-dimensional travel then it seems likely that they would be so advanced that they could find out everything they wanted to know with some kind of undetectable technology. There would be no need to come to Earth unless they were ready to make their presence known. Plus we spend billions of dollars on vast antenna arrays and electronic listening equipment to continually scan the cosmos. And so far, no one has said hello. I wonder if in a hundred years from now when we still have not received the simplest of extraterrestrial signals how we will feel about our role in the universe?

Mandi, each time you look up into the night sky, consider that you are gazing on God's backyard, His playground, and that amongst all that vastness, He has given mankind the unique opportunity to join Him in continuing to form His creation. If, that is, we can get it together enough to love and care for one another.

It seems statistically impossible that with hundreds of billions of galaxies, each with hundreds of billions of stars, that earth is the only planet on which life exists. In that big picture our conflicts seem inconsequential, and our petty existence meaningless in the overall scheme of the universe, with the exception of one thing. What if we are the only ones?

Truth, Love, and Forgiveness

I've written about the many lessons I've learned, and about the opportunities that exist even in hardship. I've written a few things that I hope made you laugh, and I've written about matters of the heart, which I've come to realize are what is truly important. But what does all that mean? Is there a point to my ramblings? Has life really taught me anything of value? I believe it has, and I can sum it up in the three most important words that ever existed—Truth, Love, and Forgiveness.

Those three simple words are so much more than mere concepts. They are the keys that open the doors to the spiritual realm. They have the power to literally bring heaven here to earth. I know this is a rather large boast, but when you consider that each of us has within us the power to create the reality in which we live, it becomes a matter of great significance. Each of us does in fact create our own reality based on our thoughts, actions, and the tools we use. The truth of the matter is that if you don't like the circumstances in which you find yourself, you have the power to change them. Truth, Love, and Forgiveness are the means in which lives are changed for the better and the spiritual journey made possible.

I wrote about choices, and somehow it always comes back to that. You must make the choice to seek out and accept these three spiritual elements. The light of Truth will illuminate your path. Love will encourage and strengthen you in order to continue when the going gets tough—and it will. And Forgiveness will allow you to keep moving forward as it provides the bridge that spans the chasms of hurt and pain that will try to inhibit you along the way. Forgiveness is the only thing that will truly help when you become immobilized in emotions like bitterness, resentment, or pain.

It probably seems like an easy concept. Who wouldn't choose Truth, Love, and Forgiveness over fear, guilt, and anger? But to live in and with these divine aspects is not that simple. Without so much as a second thought, human nature is to deny the Truth, embrace anxiety, and resent someone for even the slightest offense—let alone something serious. Whether we want to admit it or not, each of us has traveled with the unholy trinity of fear, guilt, and anger most of our lives.

When we humble ourselves to the truth it has a way of opening a person to the deepest levels of self-examination. The truth will allow you to see yourself as God sees you. The truth is the essence upon which everything is built. The universe itself literally exists on the foundation of truth. In the truth, science will find the forces that bind atoms together in order that matter can exist.

But, there is more to the truth than just its foundation principles. The Truth is my anti-ego serum. It is the antidote for the psychological toxins that the ego produces. In its presence, one cannot help but be humble. The reason for the capital T in truth is because the truth I'm referring to is the metaphysical Truth; the living spiritual entity Truth, the Spirit of righteous Holiness, the Spirit of conviction, the Truth that originates in God.

This truth is not a matter of perception. It exists much deeper than what our senses can perceive. In fact, our senses are easily fooled. A magician's slight of hand shows us that. This Truth must be embraced. It must be invited into one's being with heartfelt earnestness and prayer. It must be cherished and honored for the precious gift that it is. And most importantly it must be followed. We must learn to let our spiritual being that is connected to this Truth lead our physical being. This is what is meant by spirit led. It is the narrow gate; the path of divine destiny, the way to God.

My children perish from lack of knowledge is written in Hosea 4:6. The Truth is the key to this passage. There is no end to the mysteries that can be uncovered by the Truth. Consider that the essence of miracles lies within the Truth. When a person is so consumed and full of the Truth that they do nothing contrary to it, the Truth then manifests through that person and removes what is not God's will for that person's life. The Truth can change sickness into health, turn sadness into joy, and replace anxiety with a peace beyond understanding.

The Truth is very precious. Embrace it and your life will change.

While Love is not something that can be touched, its profound effects can certainly be felt. Yet, Love eludes scientific study. There is no meter or electronic sensor that can indicate its volume or purity. Still, no one doubts that it exists. I would step in front of a bullet to save my children simply because I love them that much.

I know what it feels like to waffle between whether God exists or whether we're on our own. But, I've come to realize that doubt as my failure to recognize that God is Love. Part of the problem is that this Love is of such omnipresent depth and infinite patience that while immersed in it we seldom take note. Does a fish consider the water in which it swims? The other part to the recognition issue is that God's love takes on many forms. For some, like me, it manifested in chastisement. Before the eyes of my heart could see clearly, my pride and arrogance needed to be dealt with, and deal with it He did. Consequently, I am forever humbled and eternally grateful.

God's discipline is not pleasant. Frankly, it is a symphony of agony, and it is the last thing I would wish upon any living creature. Nevertheless, it remains the most sacred aspect of my life. The searing pain of the truth that I needed to face felt like nothing I've ever known; yet strangely it offered life-affirming hope. Gone was my sense of yearning. Gone was the empty feeling deep in my soul. And gone was the life I'd led for forty-five years. It's difficult to explain how love came out of discipline, but it is exactly what I needed.

Your needs will differ from mine, and God will respond accordingly. If you're not too far down the road of self-absorption, it's quite possible to avoid His discipline. Maybe you only need a gentle nudge or the pruning of some excesses. But that is between you and Him. To find out, all you need do is ask Him into your life. Sincerity of heart is all that is required. So, if you're ready, invite Him in. Let

Him change who and what you are. To do this just open your heart and pray.

This is my prayer.

Dear Heavenly Father, my life is incomplete without You. I ask that You manifest in me and do what is necessary to make me whole. I ask to awaken to the divine destiny that you have waiting.

Do not take such prayers lightly. Things have already begun to change in the spiritual realm. I've come to understand that everything happens there first. It may take some time to sense His effects, six months went by for me, but when it happens, His touch will be profound.

Even though I've tried, please keep in mind, that God's activity cannot be explained in the language of man nor is it bound by space or time. Nevertheless, it is my experience that when He manifests into a person's life, you will know without a doubt that it is Him. Then, even if you are on your knees in a puddle of tears, you will begin to sense Love at a depth and volume you have never before known.

Last, but not least, you will need the bridge of Forgiveness on this journey called life. Each of us has such deep wounds caused by sin, both ours and the sins of others, that at times it seems more than we can bear. These psychological pits and fissures of pain and anger block us from spiritually moving forward. Forgiving those who have hurt you is the only way to put the seemingly impassable offense behind.

Forgiveness is both a letting go of the most wearisome burdens as well as spiritual healing. It is the only thing I have found that will heal a person's deepest injuries. Even though the body heals, without forgiveness the heart and soul do not. No one can ever be free while carrying an unforgiven burden, and God's grace is kept out of a heart filled with hate.

There is another dimension to this bridge. We are trying to reach a metaphysical destination from this physical realm. There is simply no way to do that on our own. Our goal is to enter into God's spiritual presence, but how do we do that? We need someone who has gone before us to lead the way.

Once I knew that God was dealing with me, I made no suppositions. I decided that the Creator of the Universe could direct me toward what I needed to know. It didn't take long before my newly opened heart could see that Jesus knew the way. With my sin so vivid and fresh, I began to understand what His cross truly meant.

Christ is my bridge to God; there is no doubt in my mind that He knows the way. It is through Forgiveness that each of us can find it. Christ lived forgiveness, He taught forgiveness, He healed in forgiveness, and after enduring unspeakable cruelty, His last request, given with His dying breath was, "Father, forgive them."

Jesus is our real guide on this journey. We have an opportunity to follow in His footsteps. His knowledge, His life, and His heart are all we need to climb the mountain of life and conquer the enemy within—the ego—the enemy we tolerate at great peril.

In understanding what He taught, we can learn to avoid the treacherous terrain of the self-life. Things like self-pity, self-righteousness, self-confidence, self-sufficiency, or self-absorption all lead to, believe it or not, self-destruction.

I've tried to describe forgiveness as a means to achieve a goal, that of getting closer to God. But like all things divine there is always so much more. Forgiveness goes beyond even a person's state of mind or spiritual need. I've come to experience forgiveness as a place of being. The land of forgiveness is heaven's realm on earth, and I'm never more close to God than when I'm abiding in Christ, stepping over and leaving behind my hurt and pain, and taking the medicinal truth that heals my soul. It is at those times that I enter the land of Grace and realize what God has done for me and how much Love He has for each of us.

It was during one of those times when I realized how He had answered my prayer to become a tool He could use. In His hands I had been tempered and sharpened like a plow blade that breaks the harden ground before planting. I recognized the privilege that existed in helping cultivate His land of Forgiveness. Let me assure you, I did not receive this task because of personal merit or deed. It had more to do with the fact that I needed so much forgiveness myself. Nevertheless, my destined purpose became clear, and that is to help others break the harden crust that surrounds the heart, so that each of us may enter into His grace and dwell in His presence.

So, if you're ready to accept Truth, Love, and Forgiveness into your life, you are ready to fulfill your divine nature and live in the presence of God.

F. Edward Marx   To Mandi, with Love

You Have Saved the Best Till Now

On the third day a wedding took place at Cana in Galilea. Jesus's mother was there, and Jesus and his disciples had also been invited to the wedding. When the wine was gone, Jesus's mother said to him, "They have no more wine."

"Dear woman, why do you involve me?" Jesus replied. "My time has not yet come."

His mother said to the servants, "Do whatever he tells you."

Nearby stood six stone water jars, the kind used for ceremonial washing, each holding from twenty to thirty gallons.

Jesus said to the servants, "Fill the jars with water."

So they filled them to the brim.

Then he told them, "Now draw some out and take it to the master of the banquet."

They did so, and the master of the banquet tasted the water that had been turned to wine. He did not realize where it had come from, though the servant who had drawn the water knew. Then he called the bridegroom aside and said, "Everyone brings out the choice wine first and the cheaper wine after the guest have had too much to drink; but you have saved the best till now." John 2:1-11

Mandi, you will begin so many things in life trying to offer your best. Whether a new job, a new relationship, or any new project, you will strive to present your finest. It is a time when your actions are the most ambitious, thoughtful and considerate, and each day you'll bask in the satisfaction of dipping into the vessel of your being, and providing your choicest wine.

Unfortunately, as the days progress, the essence of life will wane, and you'll have to reach deeper into yourself to fill the cup each day. With no way to replenish your enthusiasm, what remains becomes out of reach and your cup cannot be filled. Satisfaction and happiness turn to entrapment and despair; the party is over as the wine of your life begins to run dry.

But there is hope. If invited, Christ will attend. While not responsible for the empty vessel you have become, He cares so deeply for you that your request for help will never be denied. He tells His healing servants, "Fill her from my living well."

Then, as you live in His abundant realm, full of rich enthusiasm, those around you will understand—you have saved the best till now.

F. Edward Marx   To Mandi, with Love

The Last Page

A book stands in the corner,
it glows with shimmering light.
I'm drawn to look upon it,
for the story of my life.

I read each word with interest.
I laugh, sometimes I cry.
The book is so compelling,
pure truth without a lie.

The book goes by so quickly.
The pages of joy too few.
One page of hurt's too many,
But several are reviewed.

One page is all that's left now.
No writing has appeared.
A pen sits by within my grasp,
my words to choose so dear.

God fills my heart with love for all.
This page means He is near.
With pen in hand, I start to write.
Dear Lord, I have no fear....

To Mandi, with Love Order Form

Use this convenient order form when order additional copies of
To Mandi, with Love.

Please print:

Name_____

Address_____

City_____ State_____

Zip_____

Phone_____

_____ copies of books @ $11.95 each_____

Shipping @ $2.50 each_____

Total amount enclosed_____

Make checks payable to F. Edward Marx Literary Services

Send to:
F. Edward Marx Literary Services
PO Box 162
Union Lake, MI 48387-0162